The Flying Shadow

Other Handheld Classics

Ernest Bramah, *What Might Have Been. The Story of a Social War* (1907)

D K Broster, *From the Abyss. Weird Fiction, 1907–1940*

John Buchan, *The Runagates Club* (1928)

John Buchan, *The Gap in the Curtain* (1932)

Melissa Edmundson (ed.), *Women's Weird. Strange Stories by Women, 1890–1940*

Melissa Edmundson (ed.), *Women's Weird 2. More Strange Stories by Women, 1891–1937*

Zelda Fitzgerald, *Save Me The Waltz* (1932)

Marjorie Grant, *Latchkey Ladies* (1921)

Inez Holden, *Blitz Writing. Night Shift & It Was Different At The Time* (1941 & 1943)

Inez Holden, *There's No Story There. Wartime Writing, 1944–1945*

Margaret Kennedy, *Where Stands A Wingèd Sentry* (1941)

Rose Macaulay, *Non-Combatants and Others. Writings Against War, 1916–1945*

Rose Macaulay, *Personal Pleasures. Essays on Enjoying Life* (1935)

Rose Macaulay, *Potterism. A Tragi-Farcical Tract* (1920)

Rose Macaulay, *What Not. A Prophetic Comedy* (1918)

James Machin (ed.) *British Weird. Selected Short Fiction, 1893–1937*

Vonda N McIntyre, *The Exile Waiting* (1975)

Elinor Mordaunt, *The Villa and The Vortex. Supernatural Stories, 1916–1924*

John Llewelyn Rhys, *England Is My Village, and The World Owes Me A Living* (1939 & 1941)

Malcolm Saville, *Jane's Country Year* (1946)

Helen de Guerry Simpson, *The Outcast and The Rite. Stories of Landscape and Fear, 1925–1938*

Jane Oliver and Ann Stafford, *Business as Usual* (1933)

J Slauerhoff, *Adrift in the Middle Kingdom*, translated by David McKay (1934)

Amara Thornton and Katy Soar (eds), *Strange Relics. Stories of Archaeology and the Supernatural, 1895–1954*

Elizabeth von Arnim, *The Caravaners* (1909)

Sylvia Townsend Warner, *Kingdoms of Elfin* (1977)

Sylvia Townsend Warner, *Of Cats and Elfins. Short Tales and Fantasies* (1927–1976)

The Flying Shadow

by John Llewelyn Rhys

Handheld Classic 29

The Flying Shadow was first published in 1936.

This edition published in 2022 by Handheld Press
72 Warminster Road, Bath BA2 6RU, United Kingdom.
www.handheldpress.co.uk

Introduction © Daniel Kilburn and Luke Seaber 2022

Notes © Kate Macdonald and Daniel Kilburn 2022.

ISBN 978-1-912766-64-2

1 2 3 4 5 6 7 8 9 0

Series design by Nadja Guggi and typeset in Adobe Caslon Pro
and Open Sans.

Printed and bound in Great Britain by Short Run Press, Exeter.

Contents

Acknowledgements

David Murdoch, the nephew and literary executor of Jane Oliver, the widow of John Llewelyn Rees, has been a generous and enthusiastic supporter of the project to republish John Llewelyn Rees's works, and was kind enough to supply information from his own researches into his aunt's life, and his memories of her conversations about her husband. Rees family members James Anderson and Jill Alexander MBE were supportive of the project to bring these novels back into print.

Daniel Kilburn is a Lecturer in Geography and the Built Environment at University College London, where his teaching and research spans urbanism, global mobilities and social research methodologies. He is a licenced private pilot with some experience with a range of aircraft types.

Luke Seaber is a Senior Teaching Fellow in Modern European Culture at University College London. He is the author and editor of various works on British literature in the nineteenth and twentieth centuries, including (with Michael McCluskey) *Aviation in the Literature and Culture of Interwar Britain* (2020).

Introduction

BY DANIEL KILBURN AND LUKE SEABER

'*Be Air-Minded!*' This exhortation from the *Observer* on 26 July 1932 was repeatedly given to the British public in the interwar years, although rarely quite so directly as in this article headline. To be air-minded was to know about the world of aviation, of flights for pleasure, for war, for business; it was to interest oneself in technology, in celebrity aviators and aviatrices. It was to *fly*, to learn to pilot an aeroplane with an 'A' (private) or 'B' (commercial) licence; to travel for business or pleasure; to take 'joyrides' in aeroplanes at a fairground; to take flight vicariously in films, stories, poetry, posters and paintings. This hugely popular technology was operated, experienced and understood by comparatively few people, yet it had a disproportionate cultural importance. It is rare for a work of fiction to capture such a paradigm shift in its moment of ascendency, ushering the reader inside its technological, social and cultural world so deftly and compellingly as *The Flying Shadow*.

Despite the apparent ubiquity of aviation in the culture of the 1930s, there is a lack of a corresponding literary canon. English literature did not seem to have an author like Antoine de Saint-Exupéry in whom personal experience as a pilot was transmuted into novels and other works, such as *Vol de nuit* (1931; published as *Night Flight* in English in 1932) or *Terre des hommes* (1939; published in English as *Wind, Sand and Stars* in the same year). The representation of aviation in English literature of the period was largely about the experience of being a passenger or an onlooker. The experience of flying was relayed through the perspectives of non-experts, for whom the aeroplane was a mysterious machine and to whom flight meant surrendering to the expert, to the pilot. Descriptions of the mechanical, the importance of engineering and the role of the human-machine nexus are rare, as was a narrative of aviation written by someone in the pilot's seat.

This is the importance of *The Flying Shadow*, because the author John Llewelyn Rhys was above all a pilot. This is not to say that no other pilots in Britain in the interwar years wrote fiction or wrote about aviation. Two examples show how exceptional Rhys was. The first is the pilot C St John Sprigg, who is now better known by the pen-name he used to write Marxist literary criticism before he was killed in the Spanish Civil War, Christopher Caudwell. He held a pilot's licence, worked in aviation publishing and was author of *'Let's Learn to Fly!'* (1937) as well as co-author of *Fly with Me: An Elementary Textbook on the Art of Piloting* (1932). He also wrote detective novels; in *Death of an Airman* (1934) the Bishop of Cootamundra solves a murder at the flying school at which he has enrolled. This is an entertaining whodunit, and full of much valuable and accurate information on what it was like to fly and learn to fly in those years, but it is not much more than a piece of entertainment to which flying is a backdrop, however unusually expertly drawn. In contrast is T H White, best known as the author of the classic fantasy novel *The Sword in the Stone* (1938). His *England Have My Bones* (1936) is a diary of his experiences huntin', shootin' and fishin' – and flyin'. A significant part of *England Have My Bones* is taken up with White's reasonably successful attempt to learn to fly, and it contains some of the best *literary* depictions of flight from the period. But for all White's expertise in literature, he was an amateur flyer at best. *The Flying Shadow* in turn makes it clear the extent to which flying in the 1930s was in many ways considered a type of country sport – with the hunt at one point appearing below the aeroplane as 'a crowd of riders swirling down a lane as water down a gutter' (60) – a curious detail that reminds today's reader just how much we should be careful to remember that what is being described is partially a world of alien leisure pursuits to an early twentieth-century audience.

The Flying Shadow combines true expertise in aviation with being a fine novel. Rhys's first novel, out of print for over eighty years, is arguably *the* great (unknown) work in British literature to provide unrivalled descriptions of flight, and piloting, in the moment of its greatest cultural importance. This work is rare in its content and presentation by its counter to the cultural tendency, identified by social scientists, of confining activities that rely on technologically complex, confounding or concealed processes to a metaphorical 'black box' in our individual and collective understandings, inside which exist and operate things (and people) that we otherwise cannot fully know (see Latour 2007). Such a black box is symbolized, literally, in flow charts of complex systems, as a convenient black square into which run necessary inputs and from which flow useful outputs (but inside of which occur activities that need not be known). The more familiar use of 'black box' as the secure and indestructible repository of flight data and voice recordings found after aircraft crashes, to be deciphered by investigators who need to shed light on an accident, is coincidental. Yet in a way this alternative meaning is a symbolic reminder of how little can be known of the routines of flight, or how few routine lines of social or cultural enquiry seek out the unknowns of the cockpit (or the aerodrome, the hanger or club house). Researchers in science and technology have sought to open 'black boxes' and understand how human and technological elements combine in activities ranging from particle physics experiments, to power distribution grids or the manufacture of electric cars. However, the processes of piloting aeroplanes or of becoming and being a pilot remain, to varying extents, stubbornly 'black boxed' (despite the fact that there are likely many more pilots than particle physicists and that – for now – many more of us travel in aircraft than electric cars). The acts of piloting and crewing aeroplanes are fundamental in modern life (for leisure, politics, business and maintaining supply chains). Unlike other examples of black-box activities (whether the abattoir or the nuclear reactor) which we might prefer to stay hidden, society has instead maintained a voracious appetite for 'airmindedness'. It is in this context that insights gleaned from flying are all the more valuable, especially those richly contextualized in time and place, written with the assurance of an insider's perspective and inflected with subtle human observation, as Rhys does so effortlessly in *The Flying Shadow*.

From the perspective of anyone lucky enough to have taken practical instruction in flight, whether a single 'joyride' or en route to a private pilot's licence (or 'A' licence as it was then), Rhys's ability to illuminate the 'black box' of learning to fly reveals moments of recognition, however fleeting, that attest to there being something truly unique about this experience and the human relationships that flying produces. *The Flying Shadow* may leave you asking why no other novels of this kind exist, why there are so few studies of this nebulous area of flight operations. A few classic memoirs of this era have their place as required reading for aspiring aviators. While many memoirs by celebrated pilots of the period are concerned with their destinations and flight dramas, Nevil Shute's autobiography *Slide Rule* (1954) is an important technical memoir of working in British aviation design and engineering in the 1920s and 1930s. David Garnett's *The Grasshoppers Come* (1931) and *A Rabbit In The Air* (1932) record his experience of learning to fly. Ernest Gann's *Fate Is the Hunter* (1961) is a notable example, as a contemporary of Rhys, although in his compelling account the 'learning' stretches across an entire, rip-roaring, career spanning World War Two. It is harder to put one's finger on any account, whether fictional or factual, that offers such nuanced and sustained focus on the world that encompasses learning to fly; from the school (or in this case club) with its characters and conventions; to the instructors and their necessarily fluid, fleeting and yet complex relationships with each other, their ground crew and their pupils; and of course the aeroplanes and their cockpits, at once a classroom in the sky, an individual escape from earthly binds and a communion with corporeal risk (all under the 'shadow' of risking life-changing injury or death). The immediate and lasting allure of the window into this environment as it was in the 1930s may be felt more widely than by pilots or airminded types alone. For this world, so astutely studied and richly recreated by Rhys, includes all the ingredients required to bring the black box of inter-war flying training to life in all its guts and glory. This world appears fuelled as much by alcohol as by high-octane leaded gasoline, almost as novel to those who inhabited it as to the surrounding communities who sought its airmindedness second-hand, and with a cast of characters whose lives play out, often directly and painfully, under the recent legacy and prescient threat of (aerial) conflict, danger and societal upheaval. In this respect, *The Flying Shadow* is cast with such vivid definition as much from the light shone by Rhys, as by the distinctive fuselages of the de Havilland biplanes, across the landscape of inter-war Britain below.

Just as Rhys's book has long been unjustly forgotten, so too has Rhys himself. He was born John Llewelyn Rees (using the more 'Welsh' spelling for his publications) in Abergavenny on 7 May 1911. The son of a Church of England vicar, he left Hereford Cathedral School in 1929, and in 1934 he took his pilot's licence, signing up as a Sergeant Pilot in the RAF Reserve the following year. In 1936 he published his first and best novel, *The Flying Shadow*, with Faber and Faber. This brought him little in the way of fame, but did bring him something more important: among the novel's first readers was the author Jane Oliver (the pseudonym of Helen Evans). She was not only a fellow author, but also a fellow pilot. She wrote to Rhys in praise of how he had 'caught so exactly the terror and loveliness of flight' (Oliver 1941, 9). They corresponded, met, fell in love, and married in March 1939, the same year in which Rhys's second novel, *The World Owes Me A Living*, was published, once more with Faber and Faber. Happiness, as *The Flying Shadow* often suggests, did not last. The long-expected war came, and Rhys was ever more involved in RAF work. On 5 August 1940, by now a Flight Lieutenant, he was on a training flight at Harwell with Pilot Officers Arup and

Lester. Something went wrong: the Wellington bomber he was commanding stalled and dived to the ground, killing all three men (Chorley 1992, 24). Rhys had become part of the shadow that his first novel so eloquently and tragically suggests.

The Flying Shadow is the story of Robert Owen (RO to the Club members), who has much in common with his creator. Like Rhys, he is a clergyman's son from Wales; he is also, above all, a pilot, living 'for flying and flying alone' (3). After some time in the RAF – this also mirrored Rhys's life – he takes a job at a flying school, and the depiction of the world of this flying school and its people and places is the novel's triumph. We meet Hawkings, the chief instructor, a veteran pilot flying since the days before the Great War; Metcalf, who works as a test pilot for the aircraft manufacturer adjoining the flying school and who later leaves on a long-distance publicity flight; Martin, the local schoolmaster with a fondness for self-aggrandizing bragging about his (non-existent) prowess in flying; Janet Moreton, the hard-drinking trainee professional pilot; Perkins, the cynical and expert chief ground engineer; these and many others become Robert's world and the reader's close companions. As much time seems to be spent in the flying club's bar (where, as Hawkings sardonically comments, wonderful flying goes on as in the air (11), but flight remains the focus of these men and women's lives. For the instructors the mundane work of taking up those who think they may wish to learn to fly is their bread-and-butter, but always in the background is the allure of the freedom that solo flight gives, and the ever-present risk of violent and fiery death. The mundanity is buried in casual asides that work as the textual equivalent of a film scene in which a calendar's pages are shown changing at a blurringly fast rate, or posts on the Club noticeboard or the notices in the aviation periodicals devoured by the members. The very off-handedness of a report of a flight accident emphasizes how quotidian is the mortal danger the characters face: 'One of the Air Liners that used the aerodrome flew into a hill in a mist and three passengers and the pilot were burned to death' (107). It is there when the waiting Robert, Perkins and Hawkings imagine in frightening and frightened detail what will happen if a delayed cross-country flight misjudges its landing in the falling dusk and fog. It is there in the deaths of characters both major and minor.

The Flying Shadow is not only a novel of the camaraderie of flying, set against the warm lights of the saloon bar or in the harsh glare of the flames of a burning 'plane: it is also a love story. Robert gradually falls in love with Judy Hateling, a pupil of his who is married to a rich man many years her senior, a bullying figure whose off-stage presence is one of several shadows darkening the action. Another shadow is that of war – both the Great War that Robert is too young to have flown in and the vaguer shadow of a coming war that here as in so much 1930s writing is an uneasy half-felt presence. Shadows and doubts are everywhere in this novel, held only at bay, perhaps, in and by the losing of oneself in the courage and technical complexities of flight. Yet it is to flight that Robert turns to for an image as doubts gather around him even in his moments of greatest happiness:

> So it is, he thought, that even in love we live apart, shut into our own lives. As the years go by we will grow familiar with each other's tricks of speech and habits of mind, till broken phrases suffice for conversation, till an expression tells of a mood. Even then our understanding will be at the best physical, emotional, a thing imperfect, condemning us to spiritual loneliness. We shall be as two pilots flying wing tip to wing tip who, for all their nearness and understanding each of the other, can only communicate by clumsy and laborious effort. (171)

The ultimate shadow is always death, the end of flight. The tragedy that closes the novel is signposted from the title onwards; the shadow over Robert is realized in a terrible, though never truly unexpected form. Or rather, the tragedy that *almost* closes the novel. After the doom shadowing Robert comes to pass, where a more conventional novel might end, this one continues. We return, as it were, to the first chapter, where Robert played chess with his father, and in words almost identical to those that announce his departure at the book's beginning, we hear of another departure for a flying job. The novel ends (in the ambiguously ironically entitled 'last' chapter) with teaching in a life now empty of everything except the routine of flight.

The Flying Shadow is richly embedded in a sense of time and place, albeit imbued with the appropriate amount of fictional vagueness. The place is simply a 'flying club in the South of England', in the environs of the fictional small city of 'Best' (within an afternoon's reach of London by train and close enough that aircraft can fly to Hatfield for their annual certification). The time is the early to mid-1930s, as epitomized by the Club's reliance on the de Havilland 'Moth' family of light, single-engine, biplane trainers as the 'kites' making up their instructing fleet. These aircraft were fast becoming ubiquitous, as much as any aeroplane of the time, for both club training and private flying. They were basic machines, constructed lightly and predominantly from wood, with dope-covered canvas wings rigged in tension with wire, and powered by a four-cylinder, air-cooled, in-line engine (which outwardly resembles something cobbled together from a motorcycle engine parts bin). The fragility of these machines, along with their human cargo, is vividly and violently captured by Rhys's description of several crashes. In one, the 'telescoping' of the wooden 'longerons' that support the Moth's skinny fuselage is recounted matter-of-factly. The use of this technical term here aptly and chillingly brings to mind the metaphor of a telescope folding, collapsing and slamming shut around the body of the pilot ('penetrating' it as it does so with the control stick). Yet these Moths were also immensely capable machines, as epitomized in Francis Chichester's various accounts of delivering his 'Gipsy' model Moth from England to Australia in 1929, and attempting the return journey as far as Japan (Chichester

1964). He recounts frequent failures, incidents and crashes, after which his Gipsy Moth or its engine was repaired by himself and a cast of unlikely assistants (with varying degrees of engineering prowess) along the route. Indeed, comparing the flying done by Robert, Judy and the rest to the flights by Francis Chichester or Amy Johnson (who also successfully piloted a Moth to Australia), illustrates the 'banality of the extraordinary' that runs throughout *The Flying Shadow*. Today, few pilots seek out the raw thrill of open cockpit flying, where exposure to the elements leaves the pilot liable to be spattered with insects, engine oil or icy rainwater driven through the slipstream of the prop. Yet aside from the cold, there is barely a complaint about the physical endurance needed for such flying among Rhys's cast. No doubt this is realistic, for these aeroplanes were all they knew (and indeed all that would be available for such flying for some decades to come). Nor is any mention made of practicalities such as changing clothes (a tweed coat and skirt and a handbag emblazoned with a model airscrew, in Judy Hateling's case) between the mucky work of biplane flying and retiring to the civilization of the clubhouse.

What is arguably all the more remarkable about the 'banality of the extraordinary' which Rhys so poetically brings to life was the then comparative novelty of the human-machine nexus at its heart. Of course, any reader ought to approach *The Flying Shadow* knowing that powered flights were still in their infancy. The novel conveys a subtle sense of naïveté among the aviators, and a not-so-subtle 'lust of horrified interest' in the gloating spectators at a crash site (once described as a 'chorus of morons'), we hear again and again about Robert's distaste for the voracious appetite of 'every sensational newspaper' for stories of deadly accidents (81). Yet as one is ushered further into the daily routines and rhythms of flying at the Club, ever more subtle and remarkable insights into the technological and pedagogic development of 'modern' aviation may be found. For instance, flying 'blind' (whether real or simulated) by obscuring the pilot's view of the horizon and the ground (such as in cloud or fog) is as much an operational necessity at the Club as it was a global industry obsession at the time (Kilburn 2020). Robert matter-of-factly provides his students with instruction in blind flying techniques 'under the hood' (or Rhys's alternative name, 'head-in-the-bag'). This was a relatively novel procedure for the period, in which the student in the forward of the two, physically separate, open cockpits had their vision of everything except the aircraft instruments obscured by a wearable device (the hood or 'bag'), while the instructor in the rear cockpit monitored their progress and watched for hazards. Broadly similar methods of training are still used today, amounting to many dozens of hours 'under the hood' required for a commercial licence. Yet at the time, the Moth's diminutive cockpit typically included only four basic flight instruments, indicating airspeed, altitude, turn or 'slip', and engine revolutions per minute. What Rhys's contemporaries flying Moths lacked was the 'artificial horizon', still a relatively new invention that utilized vacuum pressure to spin gyroscopes behind a complex, hefty and expensive piece of instrumentation. Today, all but the most intrepid pilots of vintage aircraft rely upon this technology so routinely that it is considered as essential 'minimum equipment' for safe flight. In Rhys's day the students (for training) and at times their instructors (by meteorological necessity) could find themselves flying in 'blind' conditions with access to only the most cursory instrumentation and without the one instrument capable of actually indicating the aeroplane's position with reference to the real horizon. Today such flights would be forbidden by law and licencing restrictions, yet in *The Flying Shadow* these are routine operations in training, aerobatics and cross-country flying. Routine, that is, until conditions combine to present 'the fear of the pilot flying into some object (or the ground itself)' (75).

To fully appreciate the historical significance of the Club's flight operations, recounted as they are to emphasize their relative banality and routine more than their break-neck flying skill and the revolutionary impact of the technology, we must also consider the remarkable symmetry and synthesis with 'modern' or contemporary flight. On a technical level, this is especially true in general aviation, the starting point for most pilots, where training aircraft are typically still based on mid-twentieth century designs and technologies, which had themselves evolved from Rhys's era. While these aircraft types have the relative comfort of enclosed cockpits and an increased safety margin of a wider range of flight instrumentation and navigation and communication equipment – little else of the fundamentals of their operation have changed. Anyone who has learned to fly, or even paid more than passing attention to the process, will recognize much in *The Flying Shadow* as a narrative of learning to fly. Pilots are still taught to read the surrounding landscape, especially fields, within safe gliding distance, as Robert does, looking for favourable conditions free from ploughed furrows, pylons or trees and preferably aligned to any prevailing wind, should a forced landing be required. Equally, the procedure for an engine failure soon after take-off remains such that any pilot will recognize and hope to replicate Robert's advice to immediately push the aircraft nose down into a glide, aim for the safest landing site within a narrow arc either side of dead ahead, and never attempt a turn back to the airfield. Flying instructors still send their students solo only after around a third of the way into their training (although that amounts to rather more than the average of 15 hours' *total* flying time required for an 'A' licence in Rhys's day). Modern instructors will imagine using similar tricks of confidence to those in Robert's repertoire to prepare the student before they leave them to taxi and take-off alone, watching their solo progress nervously from the ground. By conjuring these insights from the sociology and pedagogy of flight, written with the shrewdness and eloquence of a keen observer of human relations, Rhys gives us what should have been recognized for far longer and enjoyed as a contribution of timeless importance to the teaching literature of flight. For this reason, as well as for its literary merit and sheer readability, *The Flying Shadow* deserves its place in the flight bag of contemporary pilots, alongside the likes of Gann, as prescribed reading from the early years of aviation.

Non-flying readers will derive equal pleasure from the immersive vicariousness of Rhys's descriptions of interwar flight operations, as much as from the novel's rich contextualization of time and place and shrewd observations of early flying culture and contemporary society. As an example, the juxtaposition of the novice and expert pilots, made possible by the novel's setting in a Club with an active training programme for private and commercial licencing, demystifies and humanizes the practice of flying in ways that even the most deftly crafted hero-memoirs or derring-do novels simply cannot. In this respect, Rhys makes masterful use of a learning environment as a setting in which to open the 'black box' to reveal something of how ordinary people – whether instructors, test pilots or students – are taught to do extraordinary things, undoubtedly informed by his own first-hand experience. In casting Robert as our expert guide to this world, Rhys avoids the egotistical feats of pioneer aviators of the age, which Robert himself appears to deride – 'It seemed foolish to risk security for the sake of ephemeral fame' – and with cruel prescience, as it ultimately transpires (138). Robert clearly prefers the workmanlike practice of *ab initio* training, by which method Rhys effortlessly transplants the reader into the cockpits of the Club kites. Technical terminology and operational procedures are referenced sparingly and strategically, but with fastidious accuracy, with the effect of adding a sense of double realism (the student pilots in the amateur flying club may be as flummoxed by some of the terminology as the reader). As such, the reader might soon find these rhythms and routines becoming familiar and relatable. Robert derives pure pleasure from his solo early morning 'tests' of the club kites or from grabbing some aerobatic time before tea. Climbing into bulky wartime-era flying gear, including a canvas Sutton harness and a headset for the rubber Gosport tube intercom is a laborious but essential procedure. We learn fairly quickly that the sharp air-slicing blades that the amateur calls an aeroplane propeller are what the professional calls the airscrew. After the mechanic swings this airscrew to bring the Gipsy engine to life, and as soon as it reaches temperature, the pilot 'spins up' the RPM to test the engine's performance before committing to take-off. We follow the pilots as they stall and spin, perform straight-and-level exercises, circuits and landings; find occasional opportunities for aerobatics, with rolls, loops, flicks and inversions; and, finally, return to the aerodrome, past the petrol pumps and hangers with attendant mechanics and engineers, to a parking spot on the apron. Then, with the day's work done, we stroll over to the Club with its bar, table games, briefing room and cast of sometimes unlikely and always wryly observed characters. The reader is thus deftly inducted into this world until it almost feels like we too are walking across the tarmac to a Moth, identified by the two last letters of its registration, with the imagined anticipation that we too might feel the power, sense the fear, smell the burning engine oil and ultimately take flight. Just as it was for Robert; 'the very familiarity of these things suddenly pleased him so that as he glided back to the aerodrome with the wind crying softly in the wires, he sang aloud, his words swept away by the slipstream' (16).

Beyond the rich descriptions of flight, which stand unparalleled for a novel of this era, we can discern Rhys's social observation and overt commentary, always shrewd, often cynical and at times downright scathing. Readers can be forgiven for any presumption that a seemingly 'technical' novel might be indifferent to societal concerns or cultural ruptures of the time. Rhys was, after all, a mere pilot. And the works of technically-minded contemporaries, such as Nevil Shute, instead subscribe somewhat more naïvely to a Protestant work ethic and black and white politics of 'good versus evil'. Yet Rhys (through Robert) instead appears from the outset as an initially unlikely, but ultimately incisive, commentator on the prejudices and inequalities of the times. *The Flying Shadow* levels subtle yet damning critiques of the worse vestiges of the class system and snobbery directed at Robert's (and Rhys's) Welsh roots. While Robert consciously uses an anglicized public-school accent to avoid sparring partners with a chip about the Welsh, Rhys himself used the more Welsh variant of his surname for publication. Robert also returns, at various points, to muse over the want and desperation he observes in society around him:

> I suddenly wanted desperately to explain that the people who're really brave are not the toughs who bail out of aircraft, but those who fight poverty and disease, or those who never get the one chance they want. (132)

Robert's attitude towards these and other societal ills works to subtly position social injustice alongside the sinister shadows cast by war and aerial conflict (or indeed the more immediate risk of fatal accident, career-ending medical examination or descent into alcoholism) that stalk the novel's characters. Such a commentary, if it really is present, is never forced and thus serves more to reflect the polarization of society between the emerging axes of socialism and fascism rather than bring them into focus. Other themes of the book, notable among them the role of women in aviation (and society as a whole), are handled comparatively deftly (even by today's standards) and evoke a sensitivity in Robert's (and perhaps Rhys's) gaze. The language, let alone the tone, does not leave a contemporary reader feeling uneasy beyond the conventions of the time. Yet none of this suggests a socialist inclination in Rhys's work. Robert ultimately seeks only to progress through his career through merit, to be allowed to get on with the job that he loves and which he clearly does well and, ultimately, to fly, despite any personal toll he must endure to achieve this.

The Flying Shadow is one of the most fascinating slices of 1930s life put down on paper. More importantly, it has a very good claim to being the best novel of aviation that the United Kingdom has produced. To read it is to gain an understanding of the terror and loveliness of flight that Jane Oliver and John Llewelyn Rees knew, allowing us to rediscover something of those years when the sight of an aeroplane in the sky could still engender wonder.

Works cited

Francis Chichester, *The Lonely Sea and the Sky* (1964) (Summersdale 2012).

W R Chorley, *Royal Air Force Bomber Command Losses*, volume 1 (Midlands Counties Publications 1992).

Daniel Kilburn, 'Flying Blind: The Formation of Airmindedness from a Pilot's Perspective' in Michael McCluskey and Luke Seaber (eds.) *Aviation in the Literature and Culture of Interwar Britain* (Palgrave 2020), 85–112.

Bruno Latour, *Reassembling the Social: An Introduction to Actor-Network-Theory* (Oxford University Press 2007).

Jane Oliver, Preface to John Llewelyn Rees, *England Is My Village* (Faber and Faber 1941), 7–15.

Note on the text

The text of this edition was non-destructively scanned from the first edition, digitized and then proofread. Obvious typographic and editorial errors have been silently corrected. Some words, such as 'any one', 'to-morrow' and 'some one', and a few others, have been contracted to follow modern style.

For Bettie Greenland

I too will something make
And joy in the making;
Altho' tomorrow it seem
Like the empty words of a dream
Remembered on waking.

— Robert Bridges

None of the flying schools or clubs mentioned in this book actually exists, while the persons represented are purely imaginary.

The First Chapter

1

It was autumn before the letter came. Through all the summer
he had waited, oft-times with impatience, spending the long
days swimming in the estuary, fishing for bass beyond the
bar, wandering over the sands that were flecked with bathers
and black cattle or over the deserted hills about Cader Idris,
disturbing rabbits and agile mountain sheep, hearing no
sound but the rustle of wild streams, the thin twitter of larks,
the eerie mew of buzzards and the soft insistent crying of the
wind in the short, wiry grass. At first the days were long, the
evenings after the pubs closed when he browsed among his
books, played chess with his father, or walked some giggling
girl through twilit lanes, interminable. He missed the rhythm
of Service life, the company of those living, as he lived, for
flying and flying alone.

But as the visitors drifted away and Welsh was once more
heard about the streets, as the cafés closed, the bathing
machines were hauled to the shelter of the sand dunes and
the small boats taken to a cove up-river where they would
winter pulling quietly at their seaweed-green ropes, he began
to love the idle life, paying less attention day by day to the
postman's visits, finding a strange security in the uncertain
monotony of his existence.

When the fishermen began to scrape mussels from the
river-bed with long-handled rakes he would often go out with
them, spending hazy hours on the cold water, hearing only
the rubble of the tide against the boats' sides, the splashing
of the rakes, the lilting tones of Welsh; watching the many
shades of grey. There was the grey of the mist on the fern-
golden hills, binding them into purple walls that rose tier

upon tier into the rain-laden sky. The grey of the ebbing river, the grey of the wet sandbanks where cormorants stood with wings stretched to dry, the grey of the tumbled village built haphazard up the hillside, still but for the grey strands of smoke floating tentatively upwards, the specks of children playing in the school yard. There was the grey of the oak pier, now deserted and clustered with sea-weed and barnacles. There was the everlasting grey of the rain that came with the turning tide, drifting in soft, warm, intimate from the Atlantic, sparkling on his shabby tweeds.

And as the rising tide caused them to pull up anchor and row for the mussel tanks by the lifeboat slip where the salmon nets hung listless on their frames, the fishermen would often talk of the 'great days' before the War when the slate trade was booming and the morning would find half-a-dozen sailing vessels waiting in the estuary for the wind to veer to East so that they might wing their ways to the far corners of the earth. Then it was that they grew eloquent, pausing in their quick, easy strokes to tell how wooden ships were once built on the south side of the river, of how there was a railway buried under the dunes, and drawing their rubber boots beneath their seats they would turn to point where cattle pens and a timber yard once stood.

On other days, sad West winds would blow the clouds on to the hills, the sky would be vivid blue against the sandbanks' yellow and the dunes on the opposite shore glow a dim gold in the elongated rays of the setting sun. Then he would follow the porpoise as they rolled lazily in hunting the placid river or watch the gulls who fought screaming for scraps of refuse and dropped mussels from twenty feet to break on the shore.

He carried the letter about for two days, his fingers often touching its crisp envelope, its phrases bracing his mind, before telling his father. Now that things were decided he felt a sudden disgust at his idleness, an intense desire to work again that was shadowed by the thought of the old man's resultant loneliness. They were playing chess after supper, the sibilant lamplight threading the board with grotesque shadows of the tall chessmen, bringing out the rugged character in the old clergyman's face, enlarging the cosy, book-lined room with heavy, gargantuan shadows. They had been silent perhaps an hour, only an occasional 'check' punctuating the faraway rumble of the river running over the bar at half-tide, hearing but the persistent hooting of an owl and the intermittent shuddering of the fire as it moved down in the grate, when Robert said in tones too casual to carry conviction, 'By the way, I've got a job, Father.'

He made no answer till he had moved a bishop, dragging the carved piece so that its ivory rim left a ragged path on the leather surface of the board.

'A flying job?'

He nodded, going on to explain that it was an instructor's post at a flying club in the South of England.

'I'd rather hoped you'd have tired of flying and taken something – something nearer home.'

'I'm afraid I'll never tire of flying. Besides there are no jobs going about here, and anyhow, when they learn that one's been in the Service, employers don't fall on one's neck,' he replied, thinking suddenly how his father had aged since his retirement.

'Where is this club?'

'At a place called Best. It's a long way, but I hope to get home sometimes and, of course, there'll be holidays.'

'A fortnight is a short time when taken from a year.'

'I know. I'm sorry I have to leave you.'

'That's all right, my boy. You have to work and you must do what you like. After all, it's your life. Only be careful,' he smiled, tapping his queen with a delicate finger. 'I seem to have told you that a good many times in the last six years.'

'I'll be careful,' said Robert. Was that all, he thought, did life bring no more than weariness of body as well as of spirit, no more than to sit patiently and wait for the last great experience of death? Was that all one had to look forward to, no consummation of ambition until things sought had lost their savour, no lasting strength to enjoy the pension so laboriously earned? Did one learn so little but patience, struggle towards tolerance only to become indifferent, did age teach naught but caution? Did one live through so much only to fear the future the more, was to be old, not to be wise, not to be hopeful, only to be careful? Did one live but to weary of life and become the more fearful of death?

Soon he would go through the village to the station nodding to the retired dons, soldiers, doctors and idle gentry who played with their hunting, fishing, gardening, bridge and pseudo-literary societies; shaking hands with fishermen and villagers, looking for the last time at the string of boats in the river, head to tide, the half-submerged sandbanks, thinking the while of his father in tobacco-dusty clothes, sitting in his corner, looking forward to a few years of emptiness, proud of the son who had left him to loneliness. And as he would take his ticket and when the train would ripple into motion, the river town swing from sight, the telegraph wires rock up and down before the windows, memory would net his mind.

He would remember how his world was once bounded by the high walls of the garden, by the half-understood phrases of his father and the housekeeper, by the hills of the mining valley in which they lived, hills that were then so high, so mystical, that his imagination travailed in their vastness. He would remember how first he realized his own individuality, knew in one breath-taking flash of thought (germinated in some undefinable matrix of his subconsciousness) that he was himself, understood that to find peace of mind he would have to struggle with the world, to find stillness of spirit he would have to battle within himself.

He would remember how when sick he lay awake, the firelight throwing a network shadow of the fireguard on to the nursery ceiling, the trains rattling by carrying coal to the Bristol Channel ports, while he thought of time, awed by the words of the Lord's Prayer, 'For ever and ever', thinking of eternity till his brain reeled, overwrought by the immensity of something he could only dimly comprehend. How all the lovely sadness of life seemed to be drawn into the autumn when the fern on the hillsides was golden against the October sky, when the hills themselves were a hanging wall of mist, when the air (tart with coming winter) was tinged with garden fires, when the pools in the bog over the railway were gleaming as cold lifeless eyes in the ivory moonlight.

He would remember school, the days all alike as grey beads strung upon the thread of the term. How every evening as he undressed he thought ... *I shall think of this tomorrow, remember how I undressed, folded my clothes into my basket, said my prayers and waited fearfully in my bed after the House Tutor had put out the gas (with his usual 'jokes') wondering if the others were going to beat me. I shall think of this tomorrow and another day will have passed* ... How this habit became the one reality of the day, a symbol of passing time that comforted him, its regularity introducing a sense of rhythm into the monotonous tenor of his life. He would remember how the blessed thought of the holidays increased through counted days, only to dissolve into the ennui of all but the first week at home.

How he grew older, fell shyly in love with girls in shops and trains, girls he never dared approach and seldom saw again; how he discovered Dostoievsky and would read into the nights while moths, furry and crassly determined, would

7

circle his candle till they fell burning; how he read through the nights till the chestnut trees at the bottom of the garden hung as lace against the dawning sky. He would remember the transitory, timeless dreams of pure beauty that flashed into his mind and were to him as a glimpse of the ground is to a pilot flying blind, reassuring him of his position, restoring his confidence in his navigation, lulling uneasiness so that he goes on into the damp coldness, flying happily by instruments and dead reckoning. He would remember his life in the Service. How proud he had been of his first uniform and of being saluted, he would remember the bleakness of Royal Air Force Stations, the exhilaration of learning to fly, the beauty of flight itself, the happy comradeship. He would remember...

'It's your move, my boy,' said his father gently. 'Have you been dreaming?'

2

'I had hoped', said the chief instructor whose name was Hawkings, 'to have taken you up this evening to've shown you the landmarks, but this bloody fog's covered everything.' He was a short, thick-set, middle-aged man with face beaten red by wind and rain, wrinkled about the eyes that had been screwed up against so much weather, his hands slim and fine, very white except for the tobacco stains on his square-tipped fingers. Behind his head – he was sitting on the corner of the table in the instructors' room – Robert could see a barometer, now mournfully pointing to 'Rain', which had been constructed out of an altimeter. A row of books on the ledge of the long window that looked out on to the aerodrome was supported at either end by the sawn half of a piston. Two of the walls were covered by maps, photographs and sketches of aircraft and Air Ministry Notices to Airmen, while a huge blackboard was mounted upon the third on which was chalked the record of each pupil. One door led on to the tarmac, another into the bar.

'Now, about your work here,' the other went on. 'You've been at CFS so I can't teach you anything about your job, but there are one or two things you'll find different here. In the Service you taught picked pilots a course that was paid for by the Government. Here, you teach anyone who thinks he'd like to learn to fly and has enough money to pay for it. As a matter of fact we don't teach people to fly as a rule, we shove 'em through 'A' licences. If you take too long with a pupil, and I can tell you we get some funny stuff down here sometimes, he gets upset because of the cost. On the other hand, if you get him through too quickly, the Committee get steam up because it's not bringing in enough cash. By the by, you take instructions from me and not from the Committee.

'We've three Gipsy Moths here, one with a Gipsy II fitted, and a Tiger Moth for advanced instruction in blind flying and aerobatics. As I said in my letter, I want you to concentrate on the latter side of the work. All pupils must be taught spinning before they go off solo. We start flying by testing the kites at ten. Then we go on till dusk, with time off for meals and cigarette spaces between flips. On bad days, of course, there's no flying and we have an easy day. By the by, d'you know Metcalf?'

'Metcalf?'

'Yes. He's test-pilot for Gibson's, the aircraft construction people who use this 'drome, their sheds are on the other side. He gives us a hand sometimes when we're busy. Last summer, for example, we had a scholarship scheme run by a local newspaper. He tested a lot of them for me. I should think he left the Service before you went in, he's been here some years.'

'I don't remember ever hearing of him.'

'You'll soon meet him, he's here quite a lot. Now, let's see, what else is there? Oh, about the members. There are some five hundred and thirty of 'em in the club. Of those, about a hundred are flying members and sixty-three hold 'A' licences. Thirty-one pilots fly regularly and are to be trusted. You see, on Mondays, which is our day off, those thirty-odd and only those thirty-odd, are allowed to fly. Their names are on that list behind the door. The rest have to be watched as they're eager to break their necks. All the four hundred social members do is to clutter up the bloody clubhouse, cadge flips and spend money at the bar – which incidentally keeps the club going.

'We get a few blokes who blow in, take an 'A' licence and are never seen here again, then we get people who start to have dual and give it up after a few hours, all of which brings in money. Then we've got three boys and a girl who hope to take 'B' commercial licences. They all drink too much besides being bloody awful pilots. Two of 'em will never pass the medical, but as they spend a lot of money here we don't bother to inform 'em of the fact. I'm trying to put a little polish on their piloting so that they could have a crack at the tests, but as their one idea is to split-arse before a gallery, shoot-up the bar and take friends joy-riding, it's not so easy. They haven't done their blind flying yet. I'm leaving them to you.

'Several of the Directors of Gibson's are on the Committee, so you'll probably be asked, when things are slack, to do a spot of test-piloting for the firm. You wouldn't mind, once in a while?'

'Not at all. It would be a pleasant break, once in a while.'

'Good. Then the only other thing is that you'll have to give joy-rides sometimes. I think that comprises the whole of your duty.' The elder man was silent a few seconds, looking out on to the aerodrome where the rain drifted in dim pillars over the deserted expanse of grass and limpid concrete and flapped the wind-socks about their poles.

'The only other thing I want to tell you about', he went on, 'is the way you teach people to behave in the air. Don't encourage steep turns or vertical sideslips below four hundred feet, any low flying, or aerobatics below two thousand. None of the pilots here is really good, nor flies enough to maintain a high standard. And a club isn't like the Service. A few crashes make a lot of difference in the number of people who want to learn to fly, and that makes a difference to us as instructors. One thing particularly you have to watch. As soon as pilots get their 'A' licence through, they want to go and shoot-up the home town. Very often they've done but four or five hours' solo. Their idea of impressing their friends is to fly at twenty feet or so with their heads stuck out over the side. They should crash, of course, but someone seems to look after most of 'em. It's up to you to see that your pupils don't get the chance.'

He got to his feet, dropped the paper knife which he had been jabbing into the table as he talked, and crossed the room. 'Now, unless there's anything else you'd like to know, we'll go and have one and I'll introduce you to any of the folks who happen to be in the bar.' As he swung the door open a man's voice came riding through the chatter. 'It's easy to land on one wheel, so long as you know which one's missing. You put on bank on the side that's got a wheel, increasing it as the kite becomes stalled and the ailerons gradually lose control ...'

The chief instructor grinned at Robert as he switched off the light. 'That's Martin,' he said quietly, 'he's a master at the Cathedral School with twenty hours' solo in his log book. You'll be surprised at the wonderful flying that goes on in this bar.'

3

As he walked towards the bar counter the mumbled, meaning-less conversation cloaked reality from his mind so that they all became suddenly fantastic in his eyes, the slim girls sipping gin who turned heavy glances towards him, the fat men who talked with them, one foot on the bar rail, one arm on the counter. And the lights (for they were on though it wanted some minutes to dusk) shining on the spirit bottles, the cocktail glasses, the brown arms and shoulders of the meretricious women, added to the illusion, so that he found a strange, fleeting beauty in the scene. And then, with the dread of meeting unknown people, with the knowledge that these strangers who now seemed similar in appearance and clothing, in speech and manner, would in the coming weeks evolve into individuals, upsetting his impressions, shattering hopes, belying fears, came the fading of the dream so that he saw an ordinary bar again with the familiar warm smell of beer, the aloof dexterity of the quick-moving barman, the rumble and tinkle of the cash register.

Before they were half-way across the room the conversation sagged and heads were turned, the barman pausing in his rhythmic polishing of a glass. Robert braced his mind against the rising tide of shyness that threatened to envelop his consciousness as a diver, dropping through the cool air, involuntarily braces each muscle till his body is hard and taut, anticipating the coldness of the water that rushes up to meet him.

'This', said the chief instructor, 'is Flying Officer Owen, our new instructor. Miss Anderson, one of our most enthusiastic social members.'

'How do you do?' He bowed, returning her mocking smile.

The Second Chapter

1

As Robert came out for test on the following morning he missed the unwieldy weight of a parachute flopping behind his knees with the attendant jingle of the bottom harness rings, and the feeling of being held by a uniform beneath his sidcot. The club aircraft were waiting on the apron before the hangars, their brightly doped wings rocking gently in the breeze, as huge butterflies, he thought, pinned on to the gleaming concrete. He looked about for the head GE. a small cheerful individual named Perkins, but the latter having signed out the aircraft was busy top-overhauling a motor in the workshops. Walking across to the Tiger Moth he swung himself easily into the rear cockpit. A mechanic who had been desultorily slapping paint on to a petrol pump came over, wiping his hands on cotton waste.

'Test, sir?'

He nodded, and the angular boy dived into the front cockpit to do up the loose harness. Robert eased his toes on to the rudder, watched the ailerons as he worked the stick, set the altimeter to zero and the cheese-cutter half-way forward, closed the throttle, saw that the petrol cock was open, the magneto and master switches down, did up his Sutton harness, left arm, right leg, left leg, right arm, pulled up the seat against the straps, held the stick hard back and waited for the boy to swing the airscrew. He didn't think of these things. When flying he didn't have to think.

'Petrol on, switches off, suck in, sir,' said the boy putting his hands on the airscrew. He repeated the formula and the cylinders were filled with mixture.

'Contact, sir.'

'Contact.' He pushed the starboard magneto switch up.

The boy swung the airscrew, but the motor failed to start. 'Remaining," he yelled, and jumped for the tip.

'Don't do that,' said Robert with asperity. 'Say, "off", and after the pilot repeats, pull down the airscrew till you can reach it. Then take your hands off and say "Contact", again.'

'That's not the way we swings props 'ere,' muttered the mechanic sullenly.

'It's bloody well the way you'll swing 'em when I'm in the cockpit! Now, begin again.' Morosely the boy obeyed and at the third attempt the engine started. He waited for the oil pressure to show that the motor was warm, and then motioned the boy round to hold down the tail while he tried the engine on both magnetos and up to full revolutions. This done he waved away the chocks and taxied out on to the aerodrome.

'Another muckin' RAF bastard,' said the boy to a passing mechanic. 'Thinks 'e owns the bloody 'drome. Tellin' me 'ow ter swing a muckin' prop. Me bin swingin' muckin' props for two bloody years.'

At the far end of the aerodrome he took a good look down wind, pulled down the Meyrowitz goggles that were suspended about his shabby helmet by two lengths of parachute pack elastic, turned into wind and pushing the throttle full open, eased the stick forward and then central to bring the tail into flying position. Power shivered to the nosing ribs and wing tips as the 'plane bumped and then soared upwards with that sense of smooth power that is the beauty of flight. Keeping an eye on a field into which he could force land should the motor cut, he pushed the nose down to pick up speed and then stroked back the stick till the Moth was climbing steeply. Rocking the control column laterally so that he should learn the instant the ailerons lost control and would thus be able to put the nose down before a wing should stall, he glanced down at Gibson's sheds from which a perky tractor was dragging a huge metal monoplane. By the side of the monster aircraft walked a tall figure in a white flying suit who thumbed his nose in answer to Robert's raised hand.

A good fellow, Metcalf, he thought, recalling their first meeting the previous evening; how they had spent a pleasant hour drinking and talking of pilots they had both known, types they had both flown, Service Stations, pubs and 'dromes they had both frequented, courses they had both attended. The test-pilot, it transpired, had been in the RAF during Robert's first eighteen months and although they had never met, Robert had once seen him doing aerobatics in a Bulldog at a civilian display. 'Think you'll like your job here?' he had asked, and Robert had replied that he hoped he would, 'For flying is the only thing I know.'

'Me too,' the other had answered. 'God alone knows what blokes like us did before men flew. By the way, I suppose you're fitted up with quarters and all that?' Robert explained that he had only just arrived and was putting up at a near-by pub while he looked round.

'I know of a decent little flat in the town you could get, quite reasonable too, nice district and all that. And you could take a woman there any night without any bother.'

Robert had grinned over the edge of his glass. 'Thanks. Not that women trouble me much.'

'Christ! you're lucky. Anyhow, you'd like to see it?'

'I would.'

So they had gone off in Metcalf's car, the fog heaping itself against the headlights' glare, to view the dust-ridden rooms overlooking the Cathedral Close that had charmed Robert to such an extent that he had gone to the house agent's private address to take them. And now, as he climbed towards a great grey cloud, watching the while for landmarks about the aerodrome, he thought of the furniture he would buy, the prints he would hang on the quiet walls and of how, on winter evenings, the fire-light would gleam and flicker on the backs of his books.

At three thousand feet he was above the patches of cloud that dappled the countryside with shadow, and flying level he throttled back and pushed his head over the side, memorizing the lie of the country, the compass bearings of the railways, the shapes of the largest fields. The farmers, he noticed, were growing more corn in recent years, which was to the good since stubble made an excellent forced landing surface. The district was suited to flying, having few hills and many landmarks, but pylons had been erected on the biggest fields and most of the furrows ran against the prevailing wind. A little later he began to do aerobatics, beginning with a half-roll off the top of a loop, two slow rolls and a stall turn, going on to loops and flick half-rolls and ending with a spin that finished in the damp coldness of a cloud so that he had to recover by the use of instruments.

The sight of the horizon tilting and rolling and spinning about him, the instability of the aircraft when inverted and he was hanging by the shoulder straps, the smell of burnt oil, the wind clutching the flat surfaces of his goggles as he looked over the side, the sunlight flashing back in streamers from the bracing wires and dancing in a spinning circle on the airscrew, the sound of the motor dying into shrillness in a loop, the tug of the stick in a bump, the instant response to the throttle; the very familiarity of these things suddenly pleased him so that as he glided back to the aerodrome with the wind crying softly in the wires, he sang aloud, his words swept away by the slipstream.

2

His first pupil was an unhealthy-looking Scot who wanted to put in three hours' solo flying so that his 'A' licence might be renewed. Robert spent an hour persuading him to use bank on turns and not to pull the nose up on the glide when undershooting the aerodrome, before trusting him up alone – he had done no flying for twelve months.

As he stood by the petrol pumps with helmet hanging from his shoulders by the telephone tubes, swaying goggles flashing as they caught the sun, as he watched the Gipsy Moth climb to six hundred feet, turn, fly down one side of the aerodrome, turn again, go into an uncertain glide over the gasworks and bounce over the turf on each landing, he began to think of the future, building the fabric of the coming days in his mind.

Soon the strangeness of the life would pass away, the rhythm of his work blunt the acumen with which he now saw each detail accentuated, each incident pregnant. He would find a catharsis for shyness in the steady cycle of his toil, a relief from vague intellectual questionings in the long hours of labour, the demands of patience and skill which would be made upon him.

Following the circuits of his pupil till he was certain of his safety, he thought of the thousands of times he himself would fly round the aerodrome until its approaches would become intimately familiar, until each house, each road, each path and hedge, each garden and lane, would be etched into his mind. He thought of those he would teach to fly, men and women who had never moved in freedom above the earth. How he would initiate them through the 'laying on of hands' into the smooth movements of flight, how he would encourage the quick surety of mind, the measured judgement, the calm confidence, that go to the make-up of the polished pilot.

Once again the Scot came in, held off a little too high, but made a better landing – bumping to rest within a hundred yards. He twisted his head as he taxied down wind. Robert waved him on and turned to the clubhouse where his next pupil awaited him, awkwardly concealing his nervous excitement at the thought of learning to fly.

3

The mornings grew darker so that the apse of the Cathedral was silhouetted against the dawn as he went down to the Ram for his breakfast, the great mass of the Gothic fabric fairy-like with dim and far-away lights gleaming in its lofty windows. With the coming of winter too, came the cold, for it was a hard season, so that hoar-frost lay as snow on the trim grass of the Close and preserved the tottering footprints of vergers, clergy and the few devout worshippers who attended the early morning service; while from the Cathedral School were the quick, eager footprints of the choirboys whose soulless, certain voices soaring above the soporific rumbling of the great organ, woke him each morning.

It was cold so that they wore fug boots and leather coats for flying, and the engines, which had their altitude controls disconnected, coughed and spluttered above five thousand feet. Robert, when blind-flying instructing, would sit in the icy slipstream cursing and blaspheming through the telephones, envying the pupil his warmth beneath his hood, beating his hands on the seat bearers, watching the instruments fog up and his breath floating as smoke about the cockpit.

After breakfast he would cross the Close again, usually meeting the long trail of boys returning to the Cathedral School from their daily service in the Lady Chapel. And in passing them he would do a thumbs up to Martin, now very stiff in cap and hood and gown, who would acknowledge his salute stiffly, turning away to scan the long row of pimply, shabby boys who blew on their numb fingers, talked surreptitiously or tried to trip one another up. On such occasions he seemed the perfect schoolmaster, and Robert found it hard to think of him as he was at the club, for ever bragging of his flying, giving advice on matters aeronautical so freely that he was known as 'The Ground Instructor', roaring over his Rabelaisian jokes, forever bemoaning his choice of profession. And on his free days, Robert, when passing the school later in the morning, would often hear his voice jeering, deriding, goading some small boy who struggled hopelessly with his Greek prose, would see the threatening figure, tall and shaggy in his worn plus-fours, shadowed on the florid stained-glass windows. Then the instructor would smile, remembering how stupid the master himself was at blind-flying, how many times he had to be re-told simple things, how in blind-spinning he always forgot what he had been taught, and clutched the controls, fuddled with fright.

Next, Robert would start up the old Morris Cowley he had bought for fifteen pounds and garaged in a mews behind the school laboratory and drive slowly through the city, always feeling a faint relief he never harnessed to words when he reached the outskirts of the town. At the aerodrome he would run his car into the main hangar, a privilege of Committee and instructors, and then proceed to the clubhouse, where the 'B' licence aspirants who lived on the premises would be playing with their breakfasts, blear-eyed and white-faced after the previous evening's drinking.

While the girl, Janet Moreton, was the hardest drinker of the four, she was seldom hopelessly drunk. Hardly nineteen, she was, so Hawkings said, 'definitely society'. Whatever her social origin, Robert could not but admire her capacity for pink gin and neat brandy. Every evening found her at the bar, where she would drink for hours, swopping flying and *risqué* stories with those of the social members who were treating her. The boys drank beer. One of them, a tall, well-made Londoner named Bearing, whose *suède* shoes and sophisticated manner belied his real character (he had been farming in Kenya), was a hard, natural drinker, possessed of a perfect physique that allowed him to drink all the evening and show no more than a certain lassitude about the feet. The other two, Brown and Riseling, the former thin and short, his extremely youthful appearance offset by the harsh lines about his mouth, the latter weakly, good-looking with slim, nervous hands, were made of poorer stuff. Brown, because at twenty-six he was a confirmed drunkard, and Riseling, because he thought it the thing for an airman to do, drank nightly till they leaned fuddled against the end of the bar, were sick at the corner of the car-park or indulged in loud 'Yoicks!' and cries of 'Give her six!' or 'Put this to your feet and take it, School!' tillvthe bar closed and they were taken to their rooms.

About once a week Brown would go on the water wagon and would touch no alcohol for a day or two. Then the craving would prove too strong, and Robert would come upon him at dusk slobbering kisses on some girl's arm in the back of a car, or hear him ask Hawkings, with a politeness he never displayed when sober, if he might do some night flying.

Robert's first task, after a glance at his mail and a chat with Hawkings while his goggles and helmet warmed in the sun, would be to test the Tiger Moth. The few moments of aerobatics, when he was alone and could devote himself to flying and not to correcting the spasmodic efforts of some pupil to master the elementary movements of the controls, soon came to be the happiest of the day. And coming in to land, cutting things so fine that when the wind was westerly his wheels went swishing through the grass that topped the bank by the petrol pumps, it seemed that the purpose of the day was gone and he would think as he had when a boy at school ... *I shall think of this tomorrow, remember how I brought her in for a tarmac landing, holding the wheels a foot above the ground, pulling down the tail, waiting for her to stall into a three-point landing. I shall think of this tomorrow and another day will have passed* ... And once again this habit became the one reality of the day, once more it became a symbol of passing time that comforted him, introducing a sense of rhythm into the monotonous tenor of his days.

Then the day's work would begin, the dual instruction, the careful watching of pupils who were in the embryonic stages of their solo flying, an occasional test-flight when it was good to feel seven-hundred horse-power answer the throttle once more. Sometimes there were joy-rides to be given with passengers clinging to the cockpit sides, periodically sick into the slipstream, often asking if they might return to earth before the 'plane had reached a hundred feet.

Unless things were very busy he had time for a cigarette between flips when he strolled about the apron talking to Perkins or leaned against the bar chatting to social members who had dropped in for a morning cocktail. Air liners landed regularly throughout the day, dropping their passengers at the far end of the apron, from whence they were discreetly conducted the long way round the hangars, lest their presence should contaminate club members. The pilots, mostly ex-RAF officers who flew with bored efficiency, dropped in for drinks. They lost no opportunity of bewailing their lot in having to 'bus drive for a bloody living', and would fly in any sort of weather. 'Fog?' one of them used to say, 'hang out your socks and I'll smell my way in.' When a liner happened to be empty and there was a gallery at the clubhouse, they would often stall turn one of the big aircraft, diving on the aerodrome till Hawkings, cursing loudly, would fire flares from the shelter of the petrol pumps.

On wet or windy days when there was no flying Robert would give lectures in the lounge on elementary navigation, theory of flight, rigging and engines, or have the gloves on with Bearing in one of the hangars. The latter was a good boxer with a wicked left, but always open to a right hook which was Robert's saving grace. So they were evenly matched and would box round after round, zealously timed and refereed by Perkins, who was glad of an excuse to leave his workshops for half an hour. Janet Moreton and the other 'B' licence aspirants who played badminton between the planes, would usually stop to watch them, leaning against the hangar walls, silent so that the only sounds were Perkins' ejaculated commands, the quick slapping of the boxers' feet, their hoarse, laboured breathing, the thud of glove on flesh, the flapping of the wind about the gaunt building and the rattle of the rain on its roof.

In the afternoons he would moon about the bar, play with the radio-gramophone, read the flying magazines or help Hawkings with his clerical work, filling in the 'remarks' columns of pupils' log books, dictating letters to the clerks in the control office. But for all these activities he hated the idle days, going out continually on to the rain-shiny concrete (starred with painted compass-swinging base) to look at the weather, asking Hawkings between showers to be allowed to take a pupil 'up top' for aerobatics till the chief instructor would smile at his impatience, telling him to take things easily, that he would have plenty of work to do in the future.

One November evening Robert, who had returned to the club to attend a dinner, was standing at the back of the bar. Metcalf came over to him.

'Well, RO, how goes it?' he asked, using the nickname that had clung to Robert from the first time he had initialled a bar chit.

'Oh, everything's fine. Have a drink?'

'Thanks, old man, I will. A lager, please.'

Robert ordered drinks over the heads of the girls who lined the counter.

'Well, suck in,' said the test pilot gravely.

'Cheerio.'

'How d'you like instructing, now you're settled in?'

'Very much.'

'You know, I hear you're good!'

'Do you, indeed?'

'M'm. Why don't you have a crack at an RAF Reserve flying school? Regular hours, more time off, brighter pupils, better kites, parachutes and all that.'

'I've had enough of the Service side of flying to last for a bit. Besides, I'd have to play games again, squash and rugger.'

'Good Lord! what's the matter with that? I wish I had more time to put in at golf, I only manage two rounds a week as it is.'

Robert smiled and shrugged his shoulders. 'Oh, I'm just not very keen on games, that's all.'

'You box?'

'That's not a game.'

'True. What a queer bloke you are – not being keen on games, I mean. You don't write poetry, do you?'

'No, no poetry.'

'That just gives you a pass. Same again?'

When he brought the drinks back, Robert went on thoughtfully, 'Yes, I like the work here, even though I won a prize raspberry from Hawkings this morning.'

'How come?'

'For leaving a kite on the tarmac with the motor turning while I came in to get a pupil. It's happened before. I just can't get used to petrol not being paid for by the Government.'

'You'll soon learn. How d'you get on with the chief?'

'All right. He's a nice bloke. It's some of the Committee that worry me.'

'Run foul of any of 'em, yet?'

'Not yet.'

'It'll come, and then you'll be off to that Reserve school.' He drank deeply. Robert ordered two more beers. 'Yes, Hawkings is a nice bloke,' the other resumed, 'pity he's getting beyond his job!'

'You mean –?'

'He has the hell of a job to pass his medicals for one thing. The trouble's high blood-pressure. Doctor Towsler, one of the club members, says he'd never pass him. Then his stuff's out of date, not that he isn't a damn good instructor, mind you. But, as I expect you've noticed, he doesn't know the aileron drag patter and theory and, of course, doesn't instruct in head-in-the-bag. Several of the Committee wanted to boot him out when you came and give you everything. But they've decided to keep him on till he pips his next board because of an unexpected influx of new flying members. Really, he's too old for flying, he must be well over forty. He's been flying since before the War. Learnt in the legendary days with Sopwith, and Grahame-White and Hamel and Fleming.'

'When they landed down wind with the throttle open?'

'Yes. About twenty-four years ago, when flying really was flying. When I first came to Gibson's, four years ago, he'd just given up test-piloting for them. Luckily, they were opening this place and were looking for an instructor. Mind you, he's been a good man in his time, one of the best pilots that ever split-arsed a Camel. Brought down a dozen Germans and got the MC. He had the hell of a time in France, you know, was shot down in flames and had a year in hospital.'

'I thought he'd had a bad time.'

'Why?'

'He never talks about it.'

'Yes. When it comes to the War, I'm afraid the talkers weren't the doers.' He picked up the glasses. 'Repeat order?' Robert nodded, and when he had brought back the drinks the test pilot went on. 'After the War he was in the Service for a bit and then went out to Australia and flew some of the early Air Mails. Then he went as instructor to some mid-European Air Force or other. Shook 'em up there too, I'm told. After that he came on to Gibson's and was one of the first test pilots to bail out of an uncontrollable aircraft with a parachute. At one time he'd risk anything, got an official raspberry for flying under high tension wires about fifteen years ago, but now he's too bloody careful for words. I suppose he read you the riot act about allowing pupils to muck about near the ground?'

'Rather. He fired off quite a healthy diatribe on low flying generally.'

'It's partly worry, I suppose. God alone knows what the poor blighter'll find to do when he's finished here. I hope he gets a good ground job in aviation, but I don't suppose he can pull enough wires for that.' He was silent a few seconds, knocking the bottom of his glass against a table edge. 'Makes one think, RO … Makes one wonder what's waiting for us, one day. You can't save much out of flying pay.'

'Yes,' said Robert, 'it does make one think.'

But when, a quarter of an hour later, he looked across the polished oak table, the glittering silver, through the malleable candle light, at Metcalf lost in the joyful telling of some humorous incident, heard his soft laughter through the haze of conversation, mingle with the giggle that bubbled on the painted mouth of his smooth-shouldered companion, he realized that the test pilot, as he himself, thought but little of the future, was content to live in the fulfilment of his daily task.

The Third Chapter

1

Robert had spent a Monday a few weeks later in driving through muddy lanes that held the last of the autumn in their yellow-leaved hedgerows, watching the mist rising in pools from the shallows of the rolling countryside, leaning on gates, pipe in mouth, as farm labourers, girt about with sacking, raised turnips with a rhythmic ease that belied the back-breaking nature of their endless toil, crying ragged, fierce commands to their passive, steaming horses.

He had lunched on bread and cheese and beer at a small pub some miles from Best, listening as he ate to the sorrows of the landlady whose daughter worked in a sixpenny store in the town and who had been moved to a counter by the main doors for the winter. 'Disgusting, I calls it,' she had gone on, the presence of anger in the face of one so plump giving her a ludicrous appearance. 'All the summer she was in the back of the shop, where the 'eat's something chronic in the 'ot months. Now, 'cause she won't let the bloody manager maul her about, beggin' your pardon, sir, but that's what it amounts to, she's bin moved back by the door where she was all last winter. The draught there's something cruel. It's a crying shame, sir, that's what it is.' He had contributed grunted sounds of sympathetic interest to this harangue, clearly all she expected since she had continued till he had finished his meal.

Outside the last dead leaves were drifting sadly earthwards, thudding softly against the dirty bar windows. 'My work done, I go quietly,' each one seems to say, he had thought, as it goes, brittle in death, to be blown about till it crumbles into dust, to begin once more the eternal circle of life.

And when he had driven homewards that evening the static beams of his headlights had cut a swaying tunnel in the darkness, caught the bare branches of the trees that framed the roadway, etching their lissom beauty into the black of the night, had shone momentarily on roofs soft with moss, picked out the red, stupid faces of villagers bent over handlebars or open mouthed at street corners as they paused in their conversations to be transitorily frozen in the flood of yellow light.

His flat, fireless and dusty, had seemed so cheerless and stuffy that he had given up the idea of an evening's reading and, after supper in a restaurant, had dropped into the Ram for a pint before they closed. In the bar he found Janet Moreton, unusually radiant in a black silk dance frock.

'Hullo, RO!'

'Hullo. You look very charming to-night!'

'Been all day with the aged guardian. He's just gone up to Town on the nine ten. Dinner! my dear, dinner was positively the last straw, too utterly bloody for words. I've drunk so much lemonade today, my head's whirling and my stomach's upset.'

'Drinking?'

'M'm. Pink gin, please. Why does one have to have a guardian, RO?'

'Don't know. Someone has to see that one doesn't run wild or drink, I suppose.'

'Down the hatch,' she swallowed half her gin and curled contentedly into a chair as a kitten. 'When are we going to do some night flying?'

'When we get all the flare equipment.'

'When's that?'

'In a few weeks.'

'How does one land in the dark, RO?'

'Oh, just fly on to the deck, an ordinary wheel landing, ease the stick back till the wheels touch. Then don't get it back any more or you'll take off again.'

'I see. You must give me some dual one of these days. I've never done any blind flying, you know.'

'And I've never given any dual to a woman.'

'Then I'll be one of your first victims. And talking of victims, a woman came down to the 'drome to-day asking if she could learn to fly. It was about lunch time. I was showing my guardian round. Martin was there for his morning pint and took her under his wing. Believe me, he gave her the works on flying. She thought he was an instructor. It's the joke of the place.'

'This woman, what's she like?'

'Very small, good clothes, she had a real Jaeger costume on. Lots of cash I should think.'

'I mean, what's she look like?'

'Oh, I suppose men would call her pretty.'

'And women?'

'She's not the sort to have much to do with women.'

'Looks as if I'm in for an exciting time. What happened after she thought that Martin was an instructor?'

'Oh, she just looked disappointed and said she'd come in again. The laugh's certainly on Martin at the moment!'

'Poor old Martin.'

'Don't waste any pity on that worm. He's the most unpopular fellow at the club. The way he talks and gives advice! If he were any use himself, I wouldn't say so much. And those jokes of his ... my God! and the way his Oxford manners come off when he's excited! I detest the man.'

'And I', answered Robert, when he had brought her another drink, 'rather admire him.'

'Admire Martin?'

'Yes. The confidence of the man. The way he refuses to be snubbed, goes on flying despite the minor crack-ups he's had, thinks himself the hell of a fellow.'

'When he's a lousy pilot and a nasty bit of work socially?'

'Yes. I still admire his confidence in himself.'

'D'you mean to tell me, RO,' said Janet, sitting up very straight in her chair, 'that you admire self-confidence even when the bloke who has it is someone like Martin?'

'Yes. Even when it's someone like Martin. I think it's a fine thing to have. Anyhow, the people who have the most are usually without anything to merit it.'

She drained her gin and accepted another before she spoke again. The barman began to switch off the lights to intimate that it was nearly closing time. 'You've got queer ideas, RO,' she said quietly. 'You should get drunk regularly or have a good affair.'

'I'd rather get drunk,' said Robert. 'People to-day over-estimate the importance of love.' He smiled, thinking how, as he drove her back to the clubhouse, he would slip the leather-bound tweed of his arm about her polished shoulders. How he would kiss her warm, red mouth, her slim, smooth neck. How her breath would be sweet with the smell of spirits and no word of love would be spoken.

2

After test on the following morning Robert went in to Perkins' workshop.

'JZ is flying starboard wing low, will you fix it, please?'

The GE grinned. 'Mr Hawkings complained of it last night, sir, but I waited to see what you'd say, thinkin' e might have bin sitting a bit to one side.'

'No, it's definitely down.'

'Right, Mr Owen. I'll have her in the 'angar and look her over, wants a wash-in, I expect.' He turned as a mechanic pushed the door open and threw three spanners on to the bench.

'Hey, you! easy there. Them spanners costs money, you know.'

The boy made no answer, slamming the door as he disappeared.

'Pleasant bit of work,' said Robert. 'I had to give him a raspberry on my first day here, over swinging an airscrew. He ought to have a couple of years in the Service. That would shake him up.'

'You're right there, Mr Owen. He's a good workman, I'll admit, but too much of a bloody little Bolshy for my liking. You don't catch 'is lordship puttin' in a minute overtime, no muckin' fear. 'E's not the only one neither that would be the better for a bit o' discipline. Now take the Committee of this club. There's Major Yeates, 'e may be a bit of a fool, but 'e's a gentleman, havin' bin in one of the Services like you and Mr 'Awkings. But there's that mucking Heylead, who's never done a thing but spend 'is father's money. Last night 'e comes up to me. "Perkins," 'e says, "the gentlemen's lavatory wants cleaning out," 'e says, "they smells something shocking," 'e says, "see to it, will you?" "I'm sorry, sir," I says, "but the boy's gorn 'ome and so 'ave the ack emmas." "Well," 'e says, "see to it yourself," 'e says. Me a GE with 'A', 'B', 'C' and 'D' licences, running the inspection and overhaul side of this muckin' club with never an engine missin' a rev since I've bin here. So I looks at him, but 'e nods to a broom that's in the 'angar corner and says as bold as brass, "There's a broom, Perkins," 'e says, and before Gawd, Mr Owen, for two pins, I'd 'ave stuck it up his bloody –'

'Mr Owen wanted in the instructors' room,' called a club steward from the hangar mouth.

'Duty calls, Perkins. You shall tell me again where you'd have stuck the broom, though I've a good idea.'

The bar was stale with tobacco smoke and smell of beer. Dirty glasses straggled wearily down the counter and cigarette ash smudged the coconut matting that covered the floor. Hawkings was standing at the door of the instructors' room.

'Ah, here is Flying Officer Owen. Owen, I want you to meet Mrs Hateling, a new flying member I'm entrusting to your care.' As they murmured conventional 'How d'you dos', Robert took stock of the woman Janet Moreton had been talking about. She was small, about five feet two, and wore expensive tweeds with the correct carelessness. Her hat, bag and gloves had been thrown into a heap on the map table, the gauntlets preserving the shape of her tiny hands with their lithe, pointed fingers and unstained nails. Her eyes, he noticed, were very blue. Pupils with blue eyes were reputed to make good pilots; he wondered if the saying was supposed to apply to women. She used but little make-up. Her mouth, too large for real beauty, twisted into a smile as she turned to Hawkings, who pleaded work to be done and went out on to the tarmac. Silhouetted against the sun-coated aerodrome, she watched the stocky figure of the chief instructor as he moved towards the waiting Moths, pulling taut the chin strap of his helmet. Robert noticed the clear line of her chin, the firm, slim lines of her body, her small, eager breasts and the gleam of white, even teeth as she turned towards him again.

'So you are to be my instructor?'

He nodded and said that he wanted to chat before they began flying. Would she like to sit in the bar? She smiled assent, and he dragged two chairs into the sunlight that bowed itself in through the French windows.

'So you want to learn to fly?'

She accepted a cigarette and puffed it alight, head tilted on the slim stem of her neck. 'Yes. Mr Hawkings explained that I must join the club as a flying member, told me how much the flying costs and said that the first thing to do was to get an 'A' licence.'

'I'm afraid many of our pupils never go any further.'

'Well, I want to do – to do – as much as I can.'

'Splendid. Have you done any flying?'

'Only as passenger.'

'You ride?'

'M'm.'

'Are you good?'

'Not bad. I drive a sports car, too, if that's any help.'

'It's not, really. Driving a car hasn't much to do with flying, in the same way that walking hasn't much to do with swimming. I asked about the riding because half the battle in piloting is having firm, sensitive hands.'

'How long will it take me to get an 'A'?'

'Depends on how often you come down, how regularly you come down, how you get on, and the weather.'

'If I come down every morning and the weather's good?'

'About five weeks. That's taking it easily.'

'How many hours will I have to do?'

'If you're average, about fifteen. Five of them, solo.'

'I see. When do we begin?'

'As soon as I've fitted you up with a helmet and goggles and you've signed the forms.'

Twenty minutes later they walked out on to the tarmac. Robert led her over to 'KL', the Gipsy II Moth. She walked very gracefully, he noticed, turning her feet slightly inwards. And then, as he began to explain the functioning of the controls, showing how aircraft are manoeuvred in the three planes of flight, his interest vanished and she became another pupil. He put a cushion in the pilot's seat and helped her into the cockpit. Her goggles just showed above the door. He sent a mechanic for another cushion while he explained the instruments and made her handle stick and rudder. When the cushion had been inserted he showed her the working of the Sutton harness and how to plug her telephone leads into the

Gosport tube. Then he swung himself into the front cockpit. The mechanic pulled the airscrew over and the engine started.

'Can you hear me?'

'Yes.'

'In future I want you to watch how I start and test the engine, for you'll soon be doing it yourself. Now I want you to keep your feet away from the rudder and your hands away from the stick.' As he took off he looked np into the mirror that was mounted on one of the centre section struts. Her hands were clutching the cockpit doors, her mouth set in a hard line. 'How do you like it?'

'Fine. Thank you!'

He climbed in tight circles, putting the 'plane into steep turns that brought the round shadow of his head sweeping over each lower wing in turn so that his pupil should become accustomed to the tilting horizon as the earth changed from the foreshortened familiarity of a hundred feet to the dim, map-like expanse viewed from two thousand, where the clouds became real, hard and white in their boundless beauty.

At two thousand seven hundred feet he levelled off. It was a clear, cold day with the town spread out before them, its trim streets smudged by rows of leafless trees, its slums hazy with the smoke that floated lazily for many miles to leeward. The clouds, a thousand feet above, threw rippling shadows that dappled the winter-bound landscape.

'Now,' said Robert, 'I want you to put your feet on the rudder and your right hand on the stick. At the moment I'm flying level with the nose of the machine on the horizon and I want you to follow me. If the nose drops, I ease back the stick – so. If it rises, I ease it forward – so. Again, if my right wing goes down, I push the stick gently to the left – like this – and up it comes. If my left wing goes down, I push the stick gently to the right – like this – and up it comes. Do you follow me?'

'I follow you.'

'At the same time I keep her straight with the rudder. If the nose goes to the left I put on a little right rudder – like this. If the nose goes to the right, a little left rudder. You follow me?'

'I follow you.'

'Well, you see how easy it all is? Everything done gently, no hurry, no effort. I want you to have a crack at it. I'll be ready to help you if anything goes wrong. You've got her.'

Half a mile away the Tiger Moth was looping. That would be young Brown. The young fool had one wing down as he came over the top, due to the way in which he misused his rudder. It would be a lot better for Mr Brown, he thought, if he tried to polish up his forced landings instead of messing about in an attempt to do aerobatics. This girl was going to be all right. She was very nervous, but the nervous ones made good pilots. To-day they would do more straight and level flying and then climbing and gliding and stalling. After that, back to the aerodrome for Bearing, who was to do blind take-offs. He leaned forward, putting his mouth against the green rubber mouthpiece. 'That was quite good for a first attempt. But you're holding the controls much too stiffly. Hold the stick with your fingers and relax the muscles of your forearm, put your heels on the floor of the cockpit. Sit more easily in your seat. You're making the mistake of trying to fly the machine instead of letting her fly herself. When she's trimmed with the cheese-cutter, I showed it you, it's under your left hand, she'll practically fly hands off. The last thing. When you move the stick, don't look down at it. You don't look at the gear lever when you're changing gear, do you? Keep looking at the nose of the 'plane or looking at a wing to see if it's level, or about the sky for other aircraft.'

Quarter of an hour later he had manoeuvred the 'plane over the aerodrome.

'That will do for to-day. You've put up quite a good show. Do you know where the aerodrome is from here?'

'No.'

'It's right below. You'll soon get to know the lie of the land. I've got her.' He spiralled downwards in steep gliding turns, overshot the aerodrome, side-slipped steeply left and right and dropped 'KL' for a tarmac landing.

'What a ripping landing!'

He cursed himself silently for showing off to a society woman who thought she would like to play at flying.

3

'And how', asked Riseling at lunch, 'does the charming Mrs Hateling fly?'

'She's getting on very nicely,' said Robert, helping himself to celery.

'That's what he says about everybody,' murmured Brown.

'That's what I like about him,' said Janet, 'he doesn't blab about his pupils.'

'You shall have a drink for that,' said Robert.

'I'm not drinking. I only take beer with my meals.'

'Steward! a beer for Miss Moreton, please.'

'Wait till you start blind flying, Janet,' Bearing said, leaning over for the celery. 'RO'll have a good deal to say about you.'

'If your blind flying's half as bloody as your ordinary, he's got something to say about you.'

'He's getting on very nicely,' said Robert.

'That's one in the eye for you, you intrepid birdwoman. And talking of birdwomen, where's this Mrs Hateling hail from?'

'Don't you know?' asked Brown, with his mouth full.

'I don't. But if there's anything fishy about her, l bet you do, you dirty-minded bastard.'

'Your language, gentlemen, your language,' said Janet.

'She's old Hateling's wife,' went on Brown.

'You surprise me,' put in Janet.

'How old is "old Hateling"?' asked Robert suddenly.

'Oh, he's absolutely doddering. Got one foot in the grave. Must be getting on for fifty.' Hawkings, who was lunching at an adjacent table, looked up sharply. 'He's a nasty bit of work, too,' Brown continued excitedly, 'looks like a war profiteer to me. I saw him at a dance the other night. It was the local Hunt Ball. He had her with him. She looked topping amongst all those huntin' virgins. You know the sort, RO? Horsy females who can't dance very well and have a weather-beaten mark round their necks where the stock ends. Well, as I say, Mrs Hateling looked ripping, so naturally all the lads were round. But the old boy hung about, seemed loath to let her dance with anyone. Then a bloke took her in to supper, but the old boy cut him out on the way, and my God, he gave her a look. You know, sort of "you're mine and I'm hanging on to you". And after all, the best part of a dance is that you can take a woman in your arms who wouldn't otherwise touch you with a barge-pole.'

'That's certainly one way of looking at dances,' said Janet.

'That's the only way I look at 'em.'

'What happened afterwards?' asked Riseling.

'I don't remember.'

'That was the night he was sick into a fire-bucket,' suggested Janet.

'I was nothing of the kind. I was a spot whistled, I admit, but I remember I wanted to dance with her, but hadn't the guts to risk a snub from the old boy.'

'It's a wonder she's down here,' said Janet thoughtfully.

'I don't suppose she tells him,' said Brown.

The Fourth Chapter

1

The weather, though very cold, was fine, so that Mrs Hateling was struggling with the intricacies of landing within ten days. Robert would see her yellow sports car drive up to the clubhouse as he rolled and looped on test. And coming into the bar with helmet, scarf and goggles hanging from his shoulders, he would hear her husky voice as she chatted with the 'B' licence aspirants, see her lithe figure sprawled in one of the cane chairs. She was an apt pupil and therefore all the more despondent at her failure to put an aircraft smoothly on to the ground.

'I'll never get the hang of it,' she said one morning as they went out to 'KL'. 'Either I misjudge my approach and miss the aerodrome altogether, or I hold off too soon and you save me at the last second from stalling in from thirty feet, or else I dive straight at the ground and you save me again!'

'If you don't worry about it, you'll soon get the knack. Every pilot has trouble in learning to land.'

'If only you'd tell me where to turn in and when to begin holding off, I'm sure I'd do better.'

'I want to teach you to fly, not to rely on me.'

'M'm. I hadn't thought of that.'

'Well, you can take it from me, you'll get the hang of landing any time now. Will you please get in and start her up. Then we'll go up top and do battle.'

'More landings to-day?'

'No. Spins.'

'Spins?'

He nodded, wondering whether some of the pupils had been frightening her. "There's nothing to worry about, they're quite easy. You have to do 'em before you go off solo, and then if you should ever mishandle a plane to such an extent as to spin it, you'll know what to do.' As he climbed the machine out of the aerodrome he pulled his scarf over his mouth. It was a raw, dull day with a blanket of cloud at fourteen hundred feet. 'You've got her. Carry on climbing, will you?' he shouted through the woollen covering, placing his fingers on the stick and his toes on the rudder, subconsciously following her movements as the clouds came down to meet them.

'Now a climbing turn to the left.' The nose dropped and the 'plane turned slowly to the south. He noticed that the roofs were on the new houses that bordered on the aerodrome. There were eleven players on the golf-course and a groundsman was cutting the seventeenth green.

'Now a climbing turn to the right.' Workmen were erecting a cobweb of scaffolding about the Cathedral tower. In his mind he built the scene as it would appear from his flat, seeing the knot of onlookers attracted by bustle in such quiet surroundings, heard the flat tones of command, the rattle of rope through pulley and the crash and rumble of nervous poles dragged from a writhing heap and pulled meekly aloft to be lashed into position with whistling and oaths.

'That was a shocking bad turn, Mrs Hateling. You must use more opposite rudder coming out. And I think I've told you before about looking round before going into a turn?' He looked up in his mirror as he spoke, and she nodded, her face pink with the cold. 'Right. Try another turn to the left – that's better. Now one to the right. Bank and a little rudder. Hold off bank, take off a little rudder – now you've taken it all off. That's it. Now, to come out. Opposite bank, opposite rudder. Centralize. That's quite good. You fly very well when you think about it.' Now they were near the clouds. 'Let me have her, will you? I'm going to climb through the clouds by instruments.' As he said this the mist was about them, grey, cold, clammy. 'You've never been in the clouds before?'

'No.'

'You feel the 'plane turning to the left?'

'Yes.'

'I'm afraid you're wrong, we're actually turning to the right. If you look at the rudder needle (the bottom needle on the turn-and-bank indicator), you'll see that I'm right. So now you realize why we have to use instruments for extensive cloud flying?'

He climbed in steady circles. Soon it grew lighter, much lighter, with the sun a ball of silver in the greyness, and then they shot upwards into the clear sunshine.

'I've told you before about keeping out of clouds, haven't I? If you have to fly through 'em without blind flying instruments, go through on a southerly bearing and don't try to throw the kite about or you'll be sorry for it. Now, I want you to take her again and to carry on climbing. Don't jerk the stick about so much. Find your climbing angle and stick to it, about sixty-five on the Air Speed Indicator. And one thing more, you must use more rudder in straight flying. Pick some mark on the horizon and don't let the nose stray.'

They climbed another two thousand five hundred feet before he spoke again. 'That was quite a good show, but you're still inclined to be a little stiff on the controls. Try to relax and take things a little more easily.' As he explained the theory of spinning, with engine throttled down so that the aircraft was hanging on the slots, his eyes searched the empty sky. Below, the clouds were flat as beaten snow, dazzling white in the brilliant sunshine, undisturbed except for the shadow of the Moth which slid easily, silently, over their even surface. For scores of miles there was no movement, nothing but the sunny emptiness of the sky and the hard, white floor of the clouds, the enormous silence pricked by the stutter of the engine. For the hundredth time the beauty of such a scene hooded his mind, the sense of overwhelming desolation intensifying his realization of individuality. Nothing in the world, he thought, was as lonely as this, no scene so static in beauty, so expansive in monotony.

'Now the aircraft is completely stalled. When I move the stick about the cockpit, it has no effect upon ailerons and elevators, the sound of the wind in the wires has died away. To spin I pull the stick right back and apply full right rudder.'

As the nose of the aircraft swung sharply downwards the horizon heeled till it disappeared overhead, the whiteness of the clouds whirling up to meet them. He waited till the 'plane was forced into a spiral nose-dive by the slots on the second time round and then eased on top rudder and put the stick about two inches forward. The spinning ceased, the wind moaned in the wires, the horizon dipped towards the sunlight that danced on the wide are of the airscrew. He looked up in the mirror. As he had thought, his pupil was thoroughly scared.

'That was awful. I've never been so frightened in my life.'

He laughed. 'Nonsense. You'll get used to it. You've got her. Now, climb up again and we'll do one together.'

'I don't think I –'

'You noticed how the stick is forced the way we spin. That's why, if you ease the stick straight forward, she comes out with one wing down. Do you follow me?'

'I – I follow you.'

'Right. Carry on climbing, will you?'

Again he stalled the Moth, forced it into a spin, allowed it to turn several times and then brought it out smoothly, watching his pupil's face, now white with terror, her small even teeth clenched, imagining the fine lines of her eyebrows creased beneath her goggles.

'How did you feel that time?'

'Not quite so bad – but still dreadfully frightened. It's that awful dropping feeling and everything twisting.'

'You've got her. Climb her up again and try to remember what I told you about waiting till she's level coming out of a turn, before you centralize stick and rudder. This time I want you to spin yourself. I'll be ready to help, if you should get things tied up.'

'I don't think I –'

'You remember how to come out? As soon as I give the word, top rudder and stick a little forward.'

'Y'yes.'

'Right. Do a spin to the left, will you?'

As she stalled the machine he could feel her hands and feet stiffen on the controls. Then she applied full rudder, pulled the stick right back but instinctively eased it forward as the nose dropped.

'You mustn't let the stick go forward or she won't spin,' he righted the aircraft. 'Now try again. Hold it hard back and she'll go, then wait till I tell you before you bring her out.' This time she made no mistake, and then he made her spin again and again, left and right from level flight, from gliding and steep turns, till she became accustomed to the violent motion and handled the limp controls with confidence.

'That was quite a good show,' he said twenty minutes later. 'We'll go in and land now. D'you feel all right?'

'A bit … queer.'

'It's the cold. A coffee'll soon put you right. I've got her.'

He dived the 'plane through the clouds into the grey, sunless world below, coming out some miles from the aerodrome. As they approached the hangars he asked if she felt up to trying a landing. She nodded and took over control, but her attempt was a failure, for she stalled 'KL' at thirty feet, and Robert had to dive the Moth with throttle open to save a crash. He laughed as he dropped the aircraft smoothly into the far corner of the aerodrome.

'Don't worry, Mrs Hateling. Everyone has trouble with landings.'

'I don't believe I'll ever go solo.'

'Of course you will. One of these first days, too. All 'ab initios' feel that way when they're trying to master landing.'

'About blind flying,' she continued as they walked to the clubhouse, 'I was awfully interested in what you showed me. Is it hard to learn?'

'No. Very easy, once you get the knack.'

'D'you think I could learn it?'

'Yes, I do' – he pushed open the French windows leading into the bar – 'but not for some little time yet. You really want to put in twenty or thirty hours' solo before you begin as there's quite a lot to remember.'

'In that case – I'll probably never learn. You see, my husband – isn't very keen on my learning to fly. He's in America now with a trade delegation. That's why I'm so eager to get my 'A' as quickly as possible. It'll be a great surprise for him when he returns – though, as I say, I don't think he'll altogether approve.'

'You must bring him down, and we'll show him how safe it all really is!'

'Y'yes. Though it's not that so much as –' her voice rippled into silence as the steward brought the coffee.

'Don't you tire of it? Teaching people to fly, I mean.'

'No. It's my job, and I love flying.'

'More than anything?'

'More than anything.'

'Even the same thing over and over again?'

'You soon go beyond monotony into a sort of rhythm.'

'And stupid women putting the stick forward when they should heave it back?'

'You're the first woman I've taught.'

'I wish I'd been more of a credit to my sex.'

'You're a good pupil.'

'Thank you, kind sir, but all the more to be sorry over this morning's show. I really am.'

'There's nothing to be sorry about, Mrs Hateling. Many old pilots hate spinning.'

'I shall always hate it.'

'You'll get used to it.'

'Oh. There's something I wanted to ask you about. I've used up all my flying chits, and I've read in the rules that one mustn't fly without 'em.'

'I'll get you another book –'

'But I haven't enough money with me!'

'You can give the clerk a cheque.' As he went into the instructors' room Hawkings looked up from some correspondence.

'Hullo, RO. Your next pupil's waiting on the tarmac.'

He nodded and pulled a book of five-minute chits from his locker. What the hell was the matter with the skipper, he thought, as he took the book to Mrs Hateling and picked up helmet and goggles. Surely an instructor was allowed to get out of a machine for five minutes. Turning to close the French windows, he looked back at his pupil. She had thrown off helmet, scarf and gloves and was sitting curled up in a chair, smoothing her hands about a warm coffee cup. It suddenly occurred to him that he had never realized how beautiful she was.

2

'That fellow Martin's a bloody fool,' said Brown at lunch.

'You're telling me,' murmured Janet Moreton from behind a copy of *The Aeroplane*.

'What's he done now?' asked Bearing. 'Led some buxom wench from the narrow path of virtue?'

'It's not so much what he does as the way he talks. Last night we were in the Royal Oak having a couple, and he was gassing about goin' in for a 'B' licence. Said it was a bloody silly thing to do, that pilots would soon be two a penny. When he was young, he said, chauffeurs were such a rarity you had to import 'em from France when you wanted a couple. Now the country's lousy with home-grown ones.'

'Meaning we're going to be glorified chauffeurs?' inquired Riseling.

'Precisely. And it's not as if he had such a wonderful job himself. Wet-nursing a crowd of wet-nosed kids an' crammin' Greek into 'em. Hell's Bells, what a life! Oh, and he was talking about that new pupil of yours, RO. I mean, Mrs Hateling.'

'Was he, indeed!' Robert said.

'He certainly was. It's ruddy marvellous where that bloke gets his information from. He said she's a peer's daughter.'

'I didn't know that, did you, RO?' interposed Janet.

'Not I,' he answered. 'Though she seemed –'

'Well-bred?'

'Yes.'

'Martin says she wasn't eighteen when she was married,' Brown went on. 'Apparently her mother fixed her up and she had to marry the old cod for his dough. Her family are as poor as church mice.'

'Don't forget to bring the crippled brother in!' suggested Janet.

'Throttle back, woman,' said Bearing, 'this is interesting.'

'Gosh!' said Brown, 'fancy havin' to marry that fat sod. I saw him with her at a dance –'

'You've told us that about twenty times,' cried Janet.

'Well, he's about twenty or thirty years older than she is and keeps her like a dog on a chain, Martin says, and from what I've seen, I can quite believe it.'

'What else did Martin say?' asked Riseling. 'It seems that he knows quite a lot about other people's lives. How do you feel, Janet?'

'More comfortable than you, I'm sure.'

'Martin said quite a lot. He said the old cod's never happy if she's out of his sight. But now she's cutting loose as he's in America on some trade mission or other. Martin says there'll be hell to pay when he finds out she's been learning to fly down here!'

'He'll probably shoot RO,' said Bearing. 'A pity. We shall miss our junior instructor.'

'Then I hope he does it here,' murmured Janet, picking up her magazine again. 'I'd like to be in at the death.'

3

That night the weather changed and the following days were rain-filled and harsh with wind. Mrs Hateling would wait about all day in the hope of some more instruction in landings, fretting as she played ping-pong or badminton, gossiped in the bar, watched Perkins in his workshop or listened to Robert's lectures in the lounge.

'No flying for me again to-day?' she asked a week later as he came in from test.

' 'Fraid not, Mrs Hateling. We must wait for the wind to drop.'

'I've thought so much about landing since my last dual. I'm sure I won't be able to do a thing.'

'Rot. The rest will have done you good. You'll probably be doing three-pointers right away.'

'And when I do – I'll go solo?'

'Yes. But don't worry about it. No-one goes solo in these

days until they're safe. It's not like it was when Hawkings learnt to fly.'

'How much dual did he have?'

'None.'

'None?'

'There wasn't any in those days.'

'Mr Owen? Wanted on the 'phone, sir,' murmured a steward in his ear.

' 'Lo.'

'That you, RO?'

'Surely.'

'This is Metcalf. I want you to do a job of work for me in the lunch hour.'

'Such as?'

'Aerobatics on the standard Borzoi fitted with a new type of engine.'

'I'd love to.'

'OK. Do about twenty minutes and do 'em low down over the sheds. The chief designer and staff are going to watch. I'd like the job myself, but have to take another kite back to its squadron.'

'What's the motor?'

'Oh, a new job. Only down from the works to-day. They're fitting it now. The firm say they've got the bugs out of it. They've had very satisfactory results on the bench and in the test beds.'

'I'm glad to hear it.'

'It's a seven hundred and fifty bhp motor. You ought to make a single-seat fighter talk with that in one end.'

'I will.'

'I think that's all. Oh, I'll get the designer chappie to ring up Hawkings and ask for permission for you to shoot up the aerodrome.'

'OK. Cheerio!'

'Cheerio, and thanks, old man.'

He whistled as, three hours later, he sat in Metcalf's office, adjusting a parachute harness till it fitted him tightly. It pleased him to walk on to the tarmac with bottom harness rings jingling again, to finger the twenty-odd controls as he memorized their positions, to scan the incredible number of instruments.

The engine had been started with a gas starter, and as he pulled on the Sutton harness and waited for the oil to warm up, the tall biplane rocked with the rhythm of the explosions, its streamlined interplane bracing wires flashing in the sunshine. On his right knee was strapped a small writing pad, its pages held on to the curved board by rubber bands, while the pencil attached was thrust into the top of a fug boot.

When testing the engine up to full revolutions, waving chocks away and moving slowly across the aerodrome, the 'plane swaying awkwardly as it picked its way with bursts of throttle, he became suddenly conscious of a supreme happiness at the thought of the coming aerobatics. He turned into wind, looked about him, took up the slack of his Sutton harness and pulled up the seat till the straps cut into his shoulders. Humming as he pushed the throttle wide open and the mighty engine pulled the fighter upwards into the sky, he thought how he would shortly dive at the aerodrome with airspeed touching three hundred and eighty miles an hour, how he would skim the grass and pull the aircraft into a slow upward roll, his head pressed against the streamlined rest, teeth hard together, muscles firm but not set, movements smooth and certain as he pulled the stick against the inside of his knee and then put it into the forward corner of the cockpit as his weight came on to the shoulder straps, while left hand managed the throttle and right foot counteracted aileron drag with a touch of bottom rudder.

The sense of terrible power, the earth rolling and dropping

out of sight, the calm confidence born in the conquest of fear and in the consciousness of absolute mastery that had been developed in the matrix of experience, these things would hood his mind with a strange peace. And in this peace he would find the stillness of spirit that is akin to the stillness of the body when the mind is netted by sleep, when the noises of the world are hushed, the cares of life forgotten, when the yet wakeful understanding struggles ineffectually against the fear of slipping into a lifelessness that is like the dark loneliness of death.

A little band of club members stood on the apron watching him. It was strange, he thought, how aerobatics captured almost everyone's imagination. Perhaps it was the uselessness of flying (except as a weapon of war or a means of fast and expensive transport), perhaps it was the speed and power and noise, perhaps it was the hope of seeing someone killed, that attracted them. It was strange too, how even this crowd thought of aerobatic pilots as being bravely adventurous. It was more dangerous to work in a coal mine, but miners were not heroes; it required more physical and moral courage to bear a child voluntarily, but mothers could look in vain for sympathetic interest; it was more praiseworthy, if one had the usual responsibilities, to stick to some office job, but clerks had little enough reward for so doing.

He turned and, looking down at the aerodrome which was now a tiny, untidy patch on the landscape, judged how he would do his slow rolls down wind and over the sheds. Then he swung the aircraft into wind again and throttled down to flick half-roll.

4

They stood in silence on the windswept apron, looking upwards. As the fighter dived towards them the roar of its engine deepened till the sound crashed in great waves upon their ears, introducing a sense of horrible unreality so that the gleaming aircraft, which seemed to be dropping out of the sky, had a nightmarish and grotesque aspect. At twenty feet the 'plane levelled off, dipped a little more till it seemed that the wheels were skimming the grass and then pulled up in a loop. When the fighter was standing on its tail, Robert, with a glance sideways along one wing, pressed the stick forward so that the aircraft climbed vertically upwards for many hundred feet, for all the world as a toy pulled from the floor by its string. Just before the Borzoi stalled, he eased her sharply over the top of the loop and dived out, the wind singing in the wires.

'What's that called?' asked Mrs Hateling, breaking the silence.

'A rocket loop,' Brown answered. 'Gosh! with experimental engine, too. I hope it doesn't cut out on him. I like him as a blind-flying instructor.'

'And if it did cut out?' Mrs Hateling went on.

'He'd stop flying and start a ground course on the harp,' muttered Riseling as he, with head bent back and eyes shaded, watched a half-roll off the top of a loop followed by a spin off a double flick-roll.

Again the single-seat fighter dived towards them and, when it seemed that it must crash into the hangar doors, pulled smoothly up in a slow upward roll, turning lazily on to its back as it climbed heavenwards.

Martin joined the group on the apron, his morning pint in his hand.

'Who's playing to the gallery this morning?' he asked genially.

'It's RO,' said Janet sharply, 'and he's carrying out orders. Another thing ...' her voice sagged into silence as a sail flaps loose when the cat's paw has passed.

'Well, I've seen aerobatics before,' said the schoolmaster. 'I'm going in to the fire.'

'He'll never fly like that,' Riseling said, when the other had gone.

Janet tapped her teeth with a crochet hook. When she spoke there was a note of sadness in her voice that made the others turn sharply towards her.

'We'll none of us', she said slowly, 'ever fly like that.'

The Fifth Chapter

1

It was Sunday before the weather was calm again and when Robert came in from his first lesson the steward pushed his way through the crowded bar to say that he was wanted on the telephone.

'Hullo. This is Owen, junior instructor, speaking.'

'Hullo, RO. This is Judy Hateling – what's the weather like with you?'

'Good. But it won't last.'

'Then what about a spot of dual?'

'Right.'

'When can you fix me up?'

'I can give you half an hour on landings at twelve-thirty?'

'M'm. That will do nicely.'

'Excuse me if I run along? Very busy.'

'Of course. Twelve-thirty then. 'Bye.'

' 'Bye.'

He edged through the drinkers to the instructors' room, nodding to members, refusing drinks with a smile and a quick 'This time of the day? No thanks!' pausing to speak to a tall youth with wrists as brittle as cornstalks who had been flying behind him a few moments before.

'Is it going to be all right?' asked the youth.

'I'll let you know in a moment,' said Robert, and went in to Hawkings, who was checking petrol chits.

'Well?'

'That boy, Limner, you asked me to take up!'

'Yes.'

'First of all,' said Robert, sitting on the edge of the table and accepting a cigarette, 'I asked him how much flying he'd done. He said that he hadn't been solo, but had had about five hours' dual. When I asked where he'd done it, he said, "In a friend's machine". Sounded fishy to me. Also the fact that he's down here, when his home's in Kent. Then he said that you took him up last Sunday?'

'I did. But I didn't mention it to you. Wanted your unbiased opinion.'

'Well, here it is. If that boy's ever sent off solo, he'll crash. You can teach almost any damn fool to fly, but he's beyond hope. It's not that his judgement's at fault or that he hasn't the brains. It's just that he's scared stiff and loses his head, and that's the sin against the Holy Ghost where flying's concerned.'

'Yes. I noticed all that. What did you give him?'

'Take off and turns, medium and steep. He was quite good. I'm sure he's had a lot of dual and good dual, too. Then we did spins – or, at least, I did spins. He lost his head and made no effort to get the kite out, though I bawled till I was hoarse and tried to laugh him out of fear. Had to bring her out myself three times with the pupil frozen on to the rudder.'

'And then?'

'We tried a landing. The first three times he dived straight at the deck and I pulled him out. Incidentally, he hangs on to the controls like grim death anywhere near the ground. Then the fourth time he messed his approach and got the kite stalled, cross wind, at twenty feet. Certain crash if he'd been solo.'

The elder man nodded. 'Then you think it's hopeless.'

'I do. He seems a nice lad and very keen, but he'll have to go.'

'I think the same. He put up a similar show with me last week, but I thought there might be a chance, he's very keen and then there's the money he'd spend here and the subsidy

– if he ever got a licence. Well, I suppose there'll be more trouble with the Committee. Making bricks without straw is the least they expect of an instructor.'

'Let me talk to 'em. I've never lost a pupil yet. Why should I begin now for the Committee's sweet sake?'

'You'll have plenty of chances to talk to them without bothering about this. Now, this lad. There's some mystery about him, as you say. I'm sorry, but he can't learn here. Show him in, will you, RO?'

The boy ambled to the table. Robert closed the door and walked over to the window. It was quiet on the aerodrome, the only movement the flapping of wind-socks, the perambulations of two pupils who were waiting on the apron, the roof of a car showing above the hedge as it moved down the far side of the flying field. The general atmosphere of calm urbanity was intensified by the slender tinkling of the Cathedral bells, which distance robbed of their harsh insistency.

'I'm sorry, Mr Limner,' Hawkings began, 'I'm afraid we can't teach you to fly.' The boy flushed, began to speak, hesitated. 'Both Mr Owen and myself agree that – well – you're just not suited to flying, that's all. We're both very sorry about this, but it would be dangerous for you to go on.'

'I'm willing to pay for a 'plane if I crash it!'

'That's not the point, Mr Limner. As I've said, you're not fitted for flying. Everyone is unfitted for something. After all, you weren't thinking of taking up aviation as a career, were you?'

'No.'

'Then I recommend you to give up the idea of taking a licence. I'm as sorry about it as you are, but, as I've told you, it's not your game.'

'If you won't teach me, that's all there is to it,' broke in the boy with ill-concealed emotion. 'I'll settle up for what I owe at the control office. And another thing, I'm going to learn to fly if it's the last thing I do. Good morning, gentlemen!'

2

A few seconds later Metcalf came in from the tarmac, 'Well, how's the instructing racket?'

'So-so,' said Hawkings. 'Cigarette?'

'Thanks. It's nice to come in and talk after being in that bar. I like the bar, but one gets tired, one gets very, very tired of being told how to fly. I've just been listening politely to a bloke who was telling me how much rudder to use in half-rolling of a loop. It appears that he intends doing his first solo any day now.'

'Don't look so bloody miserable,' said Robert, pulling on his leather coat. 'You've got a good job in aviation, you've got nothing to do to-day, friends like Hawkings and myself, and there haven't been any women record breakers around here for months.'

'Don't make me sick,' the test pilot answered, 'by talking about famous female pilots. That bloke you took up this morning, RO. Are you teaching him to fly?'

'Not I,' Robert said, on his way to the door. 'He's a nice enough lad, but suicidal.'

'I know.'

'You saw his effort this morning?' suggested Hawkings.

'No.'

Robert turned as he reached the door. 'Then how did you know about him?"

'That's what I came in about,' replied Metcalf, 'but since you've summed him up, there's no need to bother.'

'Go on,' said the chief instructor.

'When I was doing my last Reserve training that bloke was

at the flying school. He'd been given a commission in the RAFO from civil life. But when they tried to teach him to fly he was so dangerous that they booted him out. They were very nice about it, told him it was better to go home in a nice warm railway carriage than in a cold wooden box, and all that gag, but kicked out he was. Got in the hell of a froth about it too. Cried like a child and swore he'd learn to fly if it was the last thing he did in this world.'

'He's just told us that,' said Hawkings. 'I suppose he's gone to try another club.'

'Bloody fool,' said Metcalf succinctly.

'I don't know,' Robert's voice was thoughtful. 'In a way I rather admire him. It must be awful to be kicked out like that, with all the other blokes staying on. What would you have done if you'd been thrown out of flying when you were training?'

'Gone and found a woman!'

'What! at this hour of the day?' the chief instructor said.

'At any hour of the day or night.'

'All this is very uplifting,' said Robert, opening the door and stepping on to the tarmac, 'but I have work to do.'

'Me too.' Hawkings picked up his scarf.

'What a lovely job,' the test pilot said as he crushed his half-smoked cigarette into a froth of ash. 'What a lovely job, teaching old men and fat women to fly kites that wouldn't pull the skin off a rice pudding. Bah!'

'Bah! to you,' said Hawkings, 'and get off my bloody helmet.'

3

Mrs Hateling did five safe landings out of six that Sunday morning, but after lunch, as Robert had prophesied, the wind rose and rain dripped from the clubhouse eaves.

Searching for a magazine sometime before tea, Robert

came upon his pupil playing ping-pong with Janet Moreton. Leaning against the wall, he watched them, his eye held by the swift oscillation of the ball over the slim net, his ear soothed by the rhythmic, brittle clatter of stroke and bounce. Mrs Hateling played with a graceful dexterity that won her the game, and seeing her intent upon her play, eyes bright with desire for victory, mouth firm with determination, he remembered how in childhood, scenes such as these had been pregnant with an all but tangible beauty. He remembered how, while at school and serving with the Royal Air Force, these visions of beauty had become remoter, more ephemeral, but deeper in intellectual intensity.

And now many of the mundane causes of these spiritual ecstasies came tumbling back into his mind so that he heard again the rumble of prayers rolling and booming down Big School, the Head Master's mordant voice grinding out grovelling supplications with an aggression that defied God to take away his authority; saw once more the First Game grouped about the drinking fountain at the corner of the cloisters, faces flushed under tousled hair, damp jerseys clinging to sweat-coated, steaming bodies, the latent character in their youthful faces heightened by the naked electric lights that hastened the dying of the fog-ridden afternoon. He lived through timeless hours of aerobatics in training planes, light bombers and single-seat fighters, hours that absorbed all ambition, all sense of frustration and futility, all hope, all fear. He stood once more upon the oak pier in the village where his father lived, watching the slim, dark shape of a cargo boat come in with the dusk, her tall lights hard and meretricious against the uniform grey of the river; hearing the thud of her engines, the rustle of her screw, the lazy but insistent cries of her pilot, the twittering conversation of the small boys as they tried to read her name; sensing the shiver of anticipation that ran through the stevedores, huddled to leeward of waiting trucks, as fenders were lowered and ropes came live and quivering to their feet.

Then the dreams began to fade, so that in their fading, in the shattering of another of the fabrics that held all the beauty of his life, he strove, with familiar sense of futility, to prolong what was one experience the more, one experience the less, on the quiet journey through life.

'You look horribly worried, RO,' said Janet when the game was over.

'Doesn't he?' murmured Mrs Hateling.

'It's probably about your landings,' Janet went on.

'She lands very nicely,' Robert said.

'M'm. I got them all this morning –'

'Though some of them were wheel landings.'

'Do they count as bad ones?'

'They're quite safe, but you have to do consistent tail-down landings for your 'A' licence.'

'Well, all I'm worried about now is going solo.'

'I wouldn't worry about that if I were you,' said Janet. 'Going solo is like sex, there's not so much in it as people would have one believe.'

'There's a dreadful smartness about you, Janet,' said Robert, 'that makes me thankful I belong to the last generation.'

'But you don't. You were a small boy when the War was on, weren't you?' He nodded, and the girl went on, 'Then you belong to us!'

'Not in spirit.'

'I suppose you admire the mid-Victorians?'

'Except that they didn't fly – yes.'

'My God!'

'Can you tell me', asked Mrs Hateling suddenly, 'whether I'll get my licence within another eleven days?' Robert answered that if the weather held she should pass the tests in that time, although the licence would not be issued for some weeks. 'Good. I'm rather anxious – to finish – as soon as I can.'

4

'Have you thought how flimsy and ugly aircraft seem when they're standing on the tarmac?' he asked Mrs Hateling as they walked out on to the apron on the next morning.

'Yes. Like ships, they have to take to their medium to become things of beauty.'

'If a Gipsy Moth ever does become lovely?'

'M'm. Will I go solo to-day?'

'Depends.'

'On my landings?'

'Partly and partly on this haze. 'Fraid there's not much horizon on circuits just now,' he looked up at an almost cloudless sky that was undisturbed by a light easterly wind. 'But it should lift soon. Will you get in and start her up, please?' As he pulled on his Sutton harness and plugged his telephone tube home, he listened to her staccato commands. There was no need to worry over her flying, she ranked among the best of the pupils he had taught.

'Right. Engine's warm. Spin her up, will you?' As the Moth strained against the chocks and his eyes watched RPM and oil-pressure gauge he thought it a pity that she should so soon be giving up flying, that so apt and enthusiastic a pupil who could afford to continue, should have to throw over something which meant so much to her as soon as she gained a nominal proficiency.

She taxied slowly across the aerodrome, looking down wind as she turned eastwards. As she set the cheese-cutter and pulled down her goggles he said: 'Now when you give her the gun, do it slowly. I've told you before about ramming the throttle open.' When she took off he felt her hands stiff on the controls. She could probably smell her first solo.

'That take-off of yours is quite good, but you're inclined to put the stick forward a little too fiercely. If the ground had been very damp, the tail might have come up and bitten you. Do you follow me?'

'I follow you.'

'Another thing. Engine failure taking off. Get it into your head at once and for all that you must never attempt to turn back. If you do, you'll buy it. First because of the danger of collision with aircraft taking off parallel to you and second because you'd stall the kite on the turn. Go straight on and put her down in the best spot you can find. You can turn through as much as forty degrees to avoid direct obstacles, but you must not turn back. When the engine cuts, don't just ease the nose down as in normal forced landing procedure, ram it down like this,' he put the stick forward till the 'plane was diving steeply. 'Now in this case I'd go for that triangular field with the hay rick at the apex. You follow me?'

'I follow you.'

'Right. Carry on climbing. We'll go up top and do a spin.'

'A spin?'

'Yes. Then we'll try a landing or two. I don't think the weather will be any good for you to go solo.'

The Moth climbed steadily. It was very cold. Robert looked over one side and then over the other, interspersing commands to climb more steeply, use more rudder or keep away from the aerodrome with bursts of whistling an endless repetition of a few bars of Ravel's 'Bolero'.

'They your crowd?' he asked a few minutes later.

'Who?'

'The hunt. See them? On the starboard beam?' As she looked over the side he added sharply, 'Look after that port wing!'

'Yes. They're just moving off,' she said as she watched a crowd of riders swirling down a lane as water down a gutter, dotted about by hounds, a thread of pink coats running through them, a froth of cars and followers in the rear, all sounds absorbed by the engine. To Robert they seemed slightly ridiculous, these empty-headed bores and hard-riding spinsters, arrogant in their dignified chasing of a small stinking animal, lusting for the sight of dogs tearing a fox to shreds. But he found himself thinking of his pupil, how she, as the icy slipstream tore at her head, would be hearing the creak of saddle, the crying of hounds, the hollow rhythm of hooves, the mellow yelling of hunt servants; how she would be thinking of the excitement of the chase, smelling the rough smell of winter, feeling the damp mist blow softly against her face, riding through wet fields that held the pale sunshine in the glittering grass, past bare trees that were finely drawn on the grey background, coming home in the dusk, mud-ridden, to a fire and boiled eggs, to live again through the day's experience.

'When I suggested you coming down this morning, I didn't know it would mean you'd have to cut a meet!'

She laughed, saying there would be time to hunt again. Five minutes later she stalled the 'plane and spun to the right.

'Now!' he cried, as the Moth was forced into a spiral by the slots, and she brought the aircraft out smoothly.

'Good! Now climb up and do one to the left.'

'How do you feel now?' he asked, when she had brought the 'plane out a second time.

'Much better. I think I'm getting used to it!'

'Of course you are. Now back to the 'drome for a couple of landings.'

On her first approach she overshot considerably.

'I've got her.' He side-slipped so that the wind hee'd in the wires and Mrs Hateling was slumped into the corner of the cockpit as the familiar, foreshortened aerodrome slid up slantwise to meet them. At thirty feet he ruddered into the slip, dropped the opposite wing to check drift.

'You've got her. Try a landing, will you?'

A little nervous she pump-handled the aircraft into a wheel landing, but her next attempt was a better one, resulting in a three-pointer. After that she did three perfect landings. As the 'plane came to rest the last time he told her to taxi right back to the marking boards.

'Wait! he said as she made preparations to take-off again, knowing that as she looked up and saw his hands on the centre section struts, saw him pulling himself out of the cockpit, she would realize with fluttering heart that she was to go up alone. He chatted as he did up the Sutton harness in his empty seat, closed the front cockpit door and placed his cushion in the rear locker.

'Now take her round yourself, will you? You feel all right about it?' She answered in a whisper that she felt fine. 'You'll have to set your cheese-cutter a little further forward to compensate for the loss of my weight. Also, you'll find the machine climbing much faster. Do an ordinary circuit, and if you're worried about getting in, don't try any funny stuff, but put your engine on and go round again. Mind you come in between the marking boards and not over them.'

She nodded and he stepped back and smiled. As she took off he stood motionless, the wind hissing in the swaying end of his telephone tubes, watching the first woman he had sent up alone. She used too much rudder on the ground, but got off quite safely and climbed slowly to five hundred feet. On her first turn she used too much rudder, and he swore softly as the Moth skidded. Flying down the long side of the 'drome her engine was running too fast, in her excitement she had forgotten to throttle down to cruising revs. Then followed another turn a very bad one this time, almost all rudder. He felt a sudden qualm, wondering whether she would get slow on her last gliding turn and drop a wing with the rudder. But her last turn was perfect and she came over the boundary at thirty feet to do a wheel landing down the aerodrome. As the aircraft grunted to rest he went over.

'How was it?'

'Fair. Shockin' bad turn you did over the golf-course, and you forgot to throttle down your engine when you got to five hundred feet. Now, go and do another circuit. Look after your engine this time and remember what I told you about that rudder!'

He grinned as she pushed the throttle firmly open and flew perfectly round the aerodrome.

'I'm sorry I chewed you up after the first time round, but I do want to try and get you out of lazy habits. Now the second show was perfect,' said he as they walked to the clubhouse.

'That's all right. And now I buy you a drink?'

'That's the custom.'

She was congratulated upon all sides as she entered the bar, where an incredible number of members were waiting for the round of drinks that followed a first solo.

'Yours, RO?'

'Grapefruit, please.'

'Not a real drink?'

'Not at this time of the day, thanks.'

When she had served out a number of gins and pints of bitter she brought his drink over to the table that was set inside the corner of the French windows and commanded a view of the aerodrome.

'And how d'you feel about it all, now?' he asked.

'Rather a sense of anti-climax. I'd thought so much about it and wanted to go so much that, well, when it came, it seemed a bit tame.'

'I can understand that.'

'Will I go solo again tomorrow?'

'If the weather's good and you're quite safe when I try you out, you will. But pupils often can't do a thing when they've just been solo. You should be all right, though.'

'I was awfully frightened till I actually opened the throttle. Then there was so much to do that I didn't think about myself. Incidentally, I was most upset by the way you damned my effort with faint praise.'

'The way you used rudder on your first time round was very dangerous. It's your rudder that'll kill you if you want to break your neck. And, after all, my lecture resulted in a perfect second solo.'

'M'm. I see that now. You know,' she balanced her drink on the arm of her chair and looked intently at the fastening of her watch. 'I don't think I ever realized before what a tremendous thrill there is in being afraid!'

'Fear is the most thrilling thing in life,' he answered slowly. 'It's the afterglow that puts it above other forms of sensation. When you've been really frightened, you feel fine for days.'

'But surely you're never frightened when you're flying?'

'When I'm testing sometimes, or sending people solo.'

'I hadn't thought of that.'

They were silent and the voices of the others came in tangled sequence to their ears.

'As you put top rudder on in blind spinning you feel the kite spin the other way, though it doesn't really.'

'Did you see what C G Grey said about Farnborough this week?'

'She makes her daughter call her "Clare" and won't let the kid wear grown-up clothes. My dear, if forty ever screamed at one!'

'They're lousy kites. Like barges on the controls.'

'So I flew down and read the bloody name on a railway station board. The thing is to fly down the line at about three hundred feet, then shove your head over the side. Don't do steep turns round the joint or you'll stall in.'

She looked up suddenly. 'You set a high seal on courage, don't you, RO?'

'Yes. I do. To me, Mrs Hateling –'

'Judy.'

'Judy – courage is the greatest thing in life. This is the way I look at it. Whoever you are, whatever you do or don't do, whatever you've got or haven't got; the world will break you. Some people, like most of the modern novelists and pacifists and the Youth of the War Generation, are broken young and spend their days sitting in rooms, whining at life. Others, ordinary men and women in ordinary jobs, go out and stand up to the world. Well, it breaks them too, but it has to take so long over it that they never see it, as they never see themselves growing older from day to day.'

'Here's RO busy with the story of his life,' said Riseling, coming in from the tarmac. 'Hear you've been solo, Mrs H. Congrats … Jolly fine show.'

'Hear you've been solo,' said Brown, who was on his companion's heels. 'Stout effort, Mrs H, especially on such a cold day.'

'Thank you both. What'll you have to drink?'

'Beer, please.' The voices were unanimous.

'Well, bung ho, Mrs H, and all the luck in the world,' said Riseling a few minutes later, holding a foaming tankard aloft. When he had finished his beer and drifted back to the bar, she said:

'How old are you, RO?'

'Twenty-five.'

'You're young for such views. Have you had a tough time?'

'Not particularly. Have you?' She nodded, looking across the aerodrome and knocking the bottom of her glass against the table-edge.

The Sixth Chapter

1

After leaving the cinema, Robert lingered in the mellow glare of the facade, watching the expressions of the other members of the audience as they passed from the saccharine atmosphere of a Hollywood interpretation of pre-War Vienna, into the drab repetitive prosaicness of their own lives.

'Dreaming?'

He turned to find Metcalf grinning at him.

'Enjoy the film?'

'Yes – and you?'

The test pilot grinned again. 'Had a leg-pressing expert next to me. Otherwise OK.' He glanced at his wrist watch. 'Just time for one before they close – coming?' Some of the shops had blinds lowered over the goods, as tired eyelids, so that the sheets of cold glass held their fleeting, muffled images as they bowed their heads to the easterly wind that rasped the streets. But other windows were brightly lit, in contrast to the dim shops behind; were brightly lit so that each article, discreetly poised, displayed with all the cunning acumen of modern salesmanship, stood accentuated in lifeless brilliancy.

The bar of the Green Man was in the basement and they clattered down the hollowed steps and thrust aside the dolorous musicians who played huddled against the outside of the swing doors. Inside it was warm, thick with tobacco smoke, heavy with the smell of beer. As the doors jerked together behind them, snapping the strains of a badly-played popular song, each of the prostitutes who dallied with a half-empty glass of gin or absinthe, looked quickly, easily, sharply towards them. Each man at the bar moved his head a fraction of an inch to scrutinize them, while a barmaid swept her glance into a mirror over the inverted spirit bottles, waiting with a patience born of experience till they should walk into its compass. The men who sat drinking with their girls, or with prostitutes, the bank clerks who were making three half-pints last the whole evening, the drunken tram-driver who fumbled for the slot of a fruit machine, each of them showed a gleam of interest as the pilots walked towards the bar; so that for a second they held the attention of the whole room, silently breaking into many conversations, disturbing the sequence of many thoughts. Robert cut short his companion's protests. 'It's on me. What are you going to have?'

'A bitter, please.'

'Good evening, gentlemen,' said the barmaid as she took the order for two half-cans, 'haven't seen you lately!'

'Busy with the wife and children,' said Metcalf. 'How are things here?'

'Quiet,' said the barmaid. Her hair was striped with permanent waves, her features characterless with make- up. 'Quiet, except for week-ends.' She filled the two cans with expert jerks of the lever.

'Ninepence, please, sir'

'Well, suck in!'

'Suck in! I hear you've had an exciting day.'

The test pilot put the bottom rim of his tankard into a little bulging pool of beer and made a ring on the counter. 'Yes. Quite exciting while it lasted.' He took a long pull at his drink.

'I know they water this bloody stuff, but bottled beer's so expensive.' He paused and sighed. 'Yes. Quite an exciting day while it lasted. I was testing a new retractable undercart that some poor sod's invented. Some fool at Gibson's thought it a good thing on paper, so they fitted one to that old kite we use for engine tests. They had the hell of a job with it too. I took it up this afternoon with ballast in the back seat. After I got up I couldn't pull the wheels up, it's manually operated. Then I got 'em up and did tests and the bloody things wouldn't come down. I struggled with the handle till I nearly wrenched it off, but I couldn't budge 'em. Then, as petrol was running low, I'd only taken on enough for an hour's flying, I decided to bump the crate on to its fuselage with a dead stick. I dropped a message bag to say what I was doing, did a circuit and switched off as I came over the boards. All the lads came out to see the fun, and the fire tender was started up, not that there was any danger, but it was bound to bend the kite a bit. At about fifteen feet I had a last crack at the undercart. Of course, the damn thing came down like jam, and I did a perfect landing. They're doing some modifications to the gear now. I hope you have the next go at it!'

'Thank you.'

A paper seller stumbled into the warm intimacy of the bar. He was old, incredibly old, his age intensified by dirt, by ragged clothing, broken boots and the smile of imbecility with which he offered the sheaf of newspapers that curved to the warmth of his body.

'Now, Isaac,' called the landlord, a fat, red-faced man, sleekly shirt-sleeved, who seized with some avidity this opportunity of dropping momentarily the character of hearty, bovine urbanity which tradition required him to possess. 'Now, Isaac, outside with you. No-one 'ere wants a paper.' The old man grinned, an empty, toothless grin, and disappeared. A neatly dressed young man who sat in an alcove by the fire began to strum a Hawaiian guitar, singing softly so that the prostitutes swayed their hips to the tune as they leaned against the counter.

'You've had quite an exciting day, too, haven't you?'

'Not bad at all. To begin with, my first woman pupil went solo.'

'Oh, Judy Hateling? Good show.'

'You know her?'

'I knew her by sight before she came to the club. My Old

Boy's in steel, so's that slimy husband of hers. Gosh! I'm sorry for that girl.'

'Why?'

'Oh, the way he treats her. I heard him shout at her in a public dinner once. Everybody stopped talking. She got up and walked out. Then everyone began to talk at once.'

'Wonder she doesn't leave him.'

'Hasn't a bean of her own and her family are as poor as church mice. Again, I suppose she feels that there's enough dirty linen washed in public as it is.'

The guitar player came and stood by Robert, muttering something to the barmaid. She turned and caught the landlord's eye. He nodded. She pulled half a pint and passed it over the counter without a word.

'Didn't I hear something about a spot of bother this afternoon?' inquired the test pilot when he had ordered two more half pints.

'I expect you did. An RAF pilot turned up with his girl-friend. He'd belonged to the club before he went into the Service. Hawkings gave him permission to take the woman up. I didn't hear this as I was giving dual at the time. When I came down I could see someone split-arsing just off the deck, and thought it was Major Yeates, who's on the Committee and therefore can't be raspberried for low flying. However, the first person I saw in the bar was Yeates himself. Now by this time Hawkings was upstairs giving dual, so I dashed out to Perkins, who told me that the RAF wallah was causing all the trouble. In a few minutes he landed, and I walked out to meet him. As the woman got out of the front seat I went up to help her, and the first thing I saw was a stick in the front cockpit. The blighter'd been trying to teach his girl-friend to fly.

'Well, I started on him, but he got tough. He was a nice fellow, but wanted to impress the girl. So I had to get tough too. I found out that he'd tipped that mechanic with the sulky face – you know, the Bolshevik bloke – to put the extra stick in. I kept him talking till Hawkings came down, and then the fun started. Hawkings told him just where he got off. The bloke runs along to some of his pals on the Committee. In ten minutes Heylead was in the instructors' room. Hadn't we taken too much notice of the business, and didn't we think that we ought to apologize to the RAF wallah? It was wrong of him to have had a stick put in, but weren't we making too much of this danger stuff? After all, this fellow had done an instructor's course. 'Oh, has he?' asked Hawkings, who'd been told the same yarn. Now Hawkings had previously asked what squadron he was in, and, knowing the CO, had rung up and asked casually about the bloke, to be told that he'd only been with 'em three weeks, was fresh out of an FTS and was learning formation flying.

'Then Hawkings got busy on Heylead, and I backed him up when necessary. He was marvellous. Really the little man was grand, for all the world like a terrier ratting, and Heylead soon gave it up as a bad job. I suppose there'll be trouble in the future?'

'You bet your sweet life there will. Not about this case, of course, but there'll be trouble. You know about Heylead's brother, of course?'

'No. What about him?'

'He's a rich nitwit who dabbles in flying. Never been in the Service or anything. Took an instructor's course at some place, and Heylead's been trying to work him into the club for some time. I expect he'll get Hawkings' place, or you'll get the chief instructor's job and he'll get yours. It's only the fact that most of the Committee hate Heylead that he's not had his brother in some time ago.'

'I learn things,' Robert said, swirling the beer in his tankard, 'I learn things as the days go by.'

The guitar player was talking to the barmaid, his voice thin with a pseudo-Oxford accent.

'I did,' he said with excited jubilation. 'The other members of the concert party dared me to – so I played "Abide with Me" during a show.'

'How did you manage about the words?' asked the girl.

'Oh, managed somehow – sorry, old man!' he added quickly, as he jerked Robert's arm.

'That's all right,' he growled, and as Metcalf grinned at him he felt a sudden sympathy for this workless fool, who probably found the only happiness of his empty day in that bar, who existed in genteel poverty between concert parties and pantomimes, living emotionally for a future that he must know could never materialize. As he wondered whether to brave the derision of his companion by buying the musician a drink, the landlord began to switch off the lights.

'Time, ladies and gentlemen, please!'

2

Judy Hateling went solo again on the following morning after three landings, and Robert sent her up to two thousand feet to practise right-hand turns.

'How did it feel?'? he asked when she returned.

'Awful. I felt all right near the ground, but above six hundred feet I froze on to the controls and was afraid to look over the side –'

'You're really much safer up there, you know.'

'I know. It's so stupid of me. I'm afraid I'll never make much of a pilot.'

'Nonsense. All pupils go through these stages, only the majority of 'em pretend they don't.'

'I found my left-hand turns much better than my right.'

'That's because of all the circuits we've been doing.'

'Another thing. I still feel greatly relieved when a landing's over.'

'You'll get rid of that too, when flying becomes sub-conscious.'

'If I do enough. Will I go solo tomorrow?'

'If the weather holds.'

But the weather broke up again and Robert only gave an hour's blind flying instruction on the next morning. He spent the afternoon dealing with correspondence and playing shove halfpenny with Janet Moreton.

'Are you going to the Hunt Ball, RO?' she asked suddenly, running a scarlet nail round the edge of her coin.

'No. I'm turning in early,' he answered, intent on the passage of his halfpenny.

'Then what about the flicks or a pub crawl?'

'When?'

'Tomorrow night!'

'Busy.'

'The night after, then!'

'Busy that night as well.'

'Oh, it doesn't matter.'

'Sometime next week, perhaps. Your turn!'

3

Before tea he went out to the main hangar to fit a new plug into his Morris. Perkins, who had been adjusting the clip that held the blind flying hood over the rear cockpit of the Tiger Moth, came over to him as he ran the engine up.

'All right now, sir? I heard her missing when you drove in this morning.'

'Yes. That's cured the trouble.'

'Martin was telling you it was a valve, wasn't he?'

Robert laughed. 'M'm. I'm afraid it wasn't much of a diagnosis. Poor Martin.'

'You wasn't 'ere, sir, when 'e made the bloomer over the pilot 'oo came down to demonstrate a new kite?'

'That was before my time.'

'It was in the summer – before that muckin' Heylead threw me out of the clubhouse. I used to go in there for drinks, but 'e got me kicked out because I'm a GE, no Old School Tie and all that. You've heard the story, Mr Owen?'

'I've heard a bit about it.'

'Well, as I was saying, I was allowed in the bar at that time, and I was having one when this fellow walks in and orders a Bass. Then Martin slides up to 'im, like 'e does to everyone 'oo blows in, and starts to talk about flying. The quiet chap nods and don't say much. Martin 'ad done about ten hours then, so 'e knew all about it and started to tell the tale, telling this bloke 'ow to take off and spin and Gawd knows what. Then Mr 'Awkings comes in and bangs a chair on the floor and introduces the quiet bloke as an ex-instructor wot's demonstrating a new type of aircraft and asks if any of the 'A' licence pilots would like to fly with him. Naturally, Mr Owen, they was all as keen as mustard, but the joke of it was that Martin hadn't got 'is licence then, so couldn't go.'

And now the shadows, which had been heaped in the corners of the hangar, began to creep silently upwards, to fill the still vastness of the huge shed and to soften and then obscure the harsh lines of aerofoil, strut and bracing wire, till the 'planes were lost in darkness; to creep silently upwards till they should reach the girder-laced roof, till its grey sky-lights should themselves be dark with night.

'And yet,' continued the GE thoughtfully, 'there's something one likes about the man.'

'That's what I say.'

'Do other members agree?'

'I'm afraid not.'

'You remember that boy, Mr Owen?'

'What boy?'

'In the summer.'

'I wasn't here.'

'I forgot. In the summer, Mr Owen, we gets quite a gallery down in the evenings to watch the flying, they stands by the main gates, inside the fence. One night, one of 'em 'ad a fit or something. The strange thing was that the only one of the members 'oo cared two hoots was Martin. Fixed 'im up and took 'im 'ome in 'is car. Funny, wasn't it, sir?'

As Robert nodded assent he heard footsteps and a small figure could be seen striding' across the hangar mouth.

'You there, RO?' Hawkings' voice went rolling up into the roof. When Robert had replied he went on, 'Come out and see the fun. Is Perkins there?'

'Yes, sir.'

'You'd better come too.'

As they reached the apron Robert saw that the chief instructor was carrying a signal pistol.

'What's doing, skipper?'

'An air-taxi pilot is flying some fool of a woman down in a Puss Moth. Their ETA is four o'clock,' he looked at his watch, 'it's five to now, so he should be here at any moment.'

'The light's almost gone,' said Perkins. 'It's going to be a near thing. Is it a case of a relation coming off the hook or something, sir?'

'No. Some Society woman is creating a record by attending a Golf Dance in a different country on four successive nights. She was in Scotland last night and is going to some show in Fettington tonight. There's a reporter in the clubhouse waiting for a story. If the kite doesn't turn up soon he'll get a good one.'

'Perhaps he's landed somewhere,' Robert suggested.

'I don't think so,'? answered Hawkings, 'from the chat I had with his firm, it seems they stand to lose a good deal if he doesn't get here.'

They walked beyond the petrol pumps that were gibbeted against the approaching, mist-thickened darkness and, turning northwards, waited in silence. Soon the city clocks began to strike the hour, each hard upon another's heels as small boys running from school, and then it was quiet again and they could hear far-away laughter in the clubhouse, the clatter of a hammer on metal in one of the workshops, the sound of traffic on the main road and the rumble of Gibson's shops.

Robert thought of the pilot flying over the quiet face of England. How after long passages over moor and hill-country, fen and pasture-land, when shepherd, reed-cutter and cattle-man had watched his quick journeying bridge their sky; clean, tidy villages had come sliding into the circle of his airscrew, had passed, fallen behind, been forgotten. How he had kept his compass needle set on the 'North' of his grid ring, checked course by smoke-smeared towns, by railways, by natural land- marks. How, from time to time, he must have flown by instruments, face dulled by concentration, eyes never leaving turn-and-bank indicator, pitch and ASI. How now, he would be peering downwards through the dimness of a winter evening, glancing quickly from the obscure ground to his watch and then to the ground again, seeking a landmark, while his passenger, who shared the tiny room in the clouds, wondered with a boredom she would take little trouble to conceal, how much longer this uninteresting journey was going to last.

'There she is,' Perkins said. 'He's giving her full throttle, too.'

'I can't hear anything –' Hawkings stopped in the middle of a sentence, 'Hear it, RO?' Robert answered that he could, and that he thought the sound came from the north-east. The chief instructor nodded and fired a green light. But the sound of the Gipsy engine faded and was then lost altogether. As he fired another light the GE asked quietly how much petrol the pilot would have left.

'Can't have much,' replied Hawkings, 'because he wasn't going to re-fuel on the way.'

Then they heard the Puss Moth again, lower this time, and Hawkings fired two more lights. As the last one hissed upwards the noise of the engine deepened till Robert had an instinctive desire to duck, and the silhouette of the air-taxi could be seen as it passed a few feet above their heads.

'Shall I get the blood-wagon out, sir?' asked Perkins, but the chief instructor silenced him with a wave of his hand as he fired yet another green pyrotechnic light. Then the engine note died away as the pilot throttled back.

'Now for it,' whispered Hawkings.

It seemed, as they strained their eyes for a glimpse of the gliding aircraft, that the minute or so during which it was coming in was timeless, to be measured only in human experience. Perkins leaned forward on to his toes, sucking his breath through his teeth. Hawkings absently re-loaded his pistol. Robert counted the change in his trouser pocket, running his nail on the edge of each coin to gauge its value.

In each of their minds was the fear of the pilot flying into some object (or the ground itself). Of his seeing, too late, danger spring out of the mist, so that even the instinctive slamming of stick and throttle could not prevent the sudden unreality of a crash. And each of them pictured, as he stood in silent agony, the irregular burnt circle in the grass, littered with charred lengths of spar and longeron, with twisted wires, burnt bits of fabric, foul with fire extinguisher, with small metal fittings brightly rusted by dew. And the grass adjoining showing scores of fire-tender and ambulance tyres, beaten flat by the frenzied feet of rescuers, trodden into the earth by the sightseers who would ring the smouldering debris for many hours.

There came a sharp burst of throttle and the 'plane skimmed the marking boards, made a perfect landing and ran on into the darkness that was now settling on the aerodrome. A minute later the pilot was taxying into the hangars.

'Thanks for the fireworks,' he said, helping his passenger down the step ladder. 'I hadn't much juice and was looking for a landmark, so they helped.' They walked towards the clubhouse talking of things aeronautical.

The Society woman was a beautiful ingénue. 'It was a dull trip,' she said. 'I'm glad to have landed.'

The Seventh Chapter

1

A week of pale winter days, dreary with rain, went by before Judy Hateling flew again. Then she did an hour's solo, practising figures of eight for her Royal Aero Club Certificate tests, the passing of which entitles the holder to a pilot's 'A' licence.

'You'll do your tests tomorrow morning if the weather's good,' Robert told her when she landed. On the following morning, however, it was very hazy, so that he telephoned his pupil after he had been up on test, telling her not to come down until after lunch.

He had a busy morning, taking Bearing, Brown and Riseling up for blind flying, giving a new pupil his first lesson and taking an Oxford Groupist for a joy ride. The latter was a large, untidy, don-like figure who slapped Robert heartily between the shoulder blades, gave him his card, mentioned that he was staying at the Deanery and invited him to come in during the evening and 'have a jolly talk about Jesus Christ'.

'Lunching in town?' asked Hawkings, who had been attending a Committee meeting.

'Yes.' Robert started up his car. 'How did the show go?'

'Fairly well. I got that mechanic the sack for shoving a stick in the front cockpit the other day. I've just handed him his notice.'

'I'm sorry that he'll be out of a job, but all the same, I'm glad he's going.'

'If anything had happened to those two fools that afternoon, we'd be looking for work ourselves. By the by, be back in good time, there's some extra joy-riding this afternoon.'

'Right, skipper.'

Three-quarters of an hour later he returned, swinging his Morris through the main gates so that she rolled on the springs with tyres squealing. He noticed a strange aircraft on the tarmac with airscrew turning and wondered who had flown down in the lunch hour. Switching off his engine as he reached the corner of the clubhouse, he let the car coast over the apron and into the corner of the hangar. As he climbed out, Perkins came running towards him.

'Thank Gawd you've come, sir!'

'What's the trouble?'

'It's that kite. She's brand new. The bloke wot flew 'er down shoved off without a word. Now that bloke you said was too dangerous to learn to fly 'as turned up –'

'Limner?'

'That's 'im. 'E says he's going to take it up alone!'

'Oh, he is, is he?' Robert ran out towards the glittering aircraft. When he got within fifty yards of the 'plane he saw that Limner was already in the cockpit and that there were no chocks under the wheels.

'Hey! You –!' but his words were lost in the blast of the slipstream as the pilot opened the throttle and took off. He pulled the aircraft sharply off the ground, only easing the nose down when she was practically stalled. Then he did a wild turn at twenty feet, holding off too much bank with the nose well up.

'Gawd!' said Perkins, who had come panting up behind Robert, and then very slowly, 'as if he wouldn't die soon enough.'

'Aren't any of the Committee or Mr Hawkings about?'

'No, Mr Owen. They've all gone into town to lunch.'

'I suppose that mechanic we sacked this morning has something to do with this?'

Perkins nodded, his eyes following the aircraft. 'Do you think there's a chance of 'im getting down all right?'

Robert watched the 'plane for some seconds and then shook his head.

The aircraft, which had now reached nine hundred feet, began to climb steeply and yet more steeply. 'What the hell –?' began the GE, and then stopped as a wing went down and the 'plane began to spin with the engine on. Slowly, easily, it slipped downwards in a tight circle as gracefully as a dead leaf fluttering earthwards. Then came the roar of the crash and silence.

'Riseling!' roared Robert as the former came running out of the clubhouse, 'ring up Dr Towsler, his number's on the emergency board in the instructors' room. Tell him there's been a bad crash a mile north-east of the aerodrome and ask him to get there as quickly as he can! Perkins! take the blood-wagon – will you?' He ran to the fire-tender, swung himself into the driver's seat, started and raced the cold engine. As the gears bit and he moved out of the hangar he saw Bearing with two of the mechanics running up the tarmac and, slowing down, motioned them to jump aboard. Turning on to the main road, the back of the tender began to slide against the camber. He swore softly and wrenched the front wheels into the crab-wise motion, killing the skid before it developed. Looking into the mirror he could see Perkins in the tall ambulance hard behind.

Half a mile down the road one of the mechanics began to beat his hands on the roof of the driver's cab. Robert took his foot off the throttle and heard the boy say that the 'plane had crashed into a field on his left. Bearing jumped over the tail-board to open the gate and when Robert drove the tender slithering through the shiny mud, he noticed a familiar yellow sports car drawn up, empty, at the roadside.

The aircraft had spun into the far corner of the field and as the heavy lorry bumped over the grass he took stock of the damage. Both blades of the airscrew were broken off, the wings were crumpled and only held together by sagging pools of doped fabric. The engine had been torn from its bearers by the force of the impact and lay battered and untidy, some yards away. The main petrol tank had burst, but by a miracle the wreckage had not caught fire.

He pulled the tender up some distance from the crash, seized an axe, small fire extinguisher, sheath knife and hacksaw and ran towards the crumpled fuselage.

Judy Hateling was leaning over the cockpit, trying desperately to lift the pilot's broken body.

'Don't pull him out!' said Robert quietly, 'we'll have to cut the longerons away.' He began to slash at the fabric. Perkins came up and started to pump fire extinguisher over the petrol-soaked debris. Judy moved away. Her face was white, stupid with fright and anguish, her light tweed coat stained with a large, dark pool of blood.

The pilot's face was grey with death. He had been trapped by the telescoping of the longerons, the stick had penetrated his stomach and his feet were entangled in a mass of wreckage that had been the front cockpit. Robert worked with deft surety, sawing away longerons, hacking at broken cockpit doors and the splintered instrument board, shouting to the mechanics to stop smoking among the sightseers who were already swarming across the field.

He hated the experience for its melodramatic propensities, the scene for its unreality. He loathed the lust of horrified interest which brought more and more spectators to gloat over the dying boy who became partially conscious, writhing and moaning as Robert strove to free him. He felt a sudden nausea at the thought of hearing again and again the story of the crash, the eye-witness phrase-perfect, pausing for the exclamations of horror which experience would teach him to anticipate, his tale smooth with many tellings, bringing delight to those so blasé that only sudden death could thrill them. He thought, as he ripped and tore with frenzied method, of the reporters who would pester any witness of the accident, fight for turns at the telephone in the control office; of their editors who would splash this splendid story, fully illustrated, into every sensational newspaper. ('Mrs Limner, on being informed of her son's death by our reporter, showed considerable emotion. 'I knew this flying would be the death of him,' she said with tears brimming her eyes.') Then there would be an inquest with supercilious coroner, nervous witnesses contradicting each other's evidence, reporters lusting for further sensationalism, weeping relatives, kindly, thick-headed policemen. And through all these things the ever-present unreality, emanating from the shock which broke down, for a little time, the conventions that wall men's minds.

In a little while Hawkings came up, and after him the doctor. Between them they got the boy on to the stretcher. He was badly broken up, and the doctor said that there was little chance of his living. As they lifted him into the ambulance he had another haemorrhage and died, the crowd pressing about him.

2

While the chief instructor issued instructions for the removal of the debris, Robert pushed his way through the crowd, searching for Judy. He nodded to Bearing, who was chatting to a tramp.

'Hawful,' the latter was saying. 'I wouldn't go up in one of them things for a fortune.'

'Why not?' Bearing asked. 'Other things are dangerous besides flying!'

"E probably thought that, too,' the tramp jerked his head towards the ambulance. 'But now 'e's dead and 'tis sweet to live.'

'Seen Mrs Hateling?'? asked Robert. The pupil answered that he thought he had seen her sitting in her car by the gate when he had gone back to help the doctor get his Alvis through the mud. Robert thanked him and pushed through the crowd again. Souvenir hunting had begun, and he heard a mechanic arguing with a fat man, who was trying to lever a pitot head from an interplane strut with his pocket knife. Hawkings caught his arm.

'Seen Mrs Hateling?'

'I'm looking for her. Just heard she's in her car by the gate.'

'How did she get mixed up in this?'

'She was here when we arrived. Must have seen it happen as she was passing.'

'Too bad. It's knocked her to bits by the look of it. See she gets home all right, will you? Then come back to the 'drome. We'll have to have a confab over this.'

'Right, skipper.'

He found her crumpled into a corner of the driving seat, crying bitterly. Two little girls were standing hand in hand in the road, watching her with solemn interest.

When he asked if he should drive her home, she nodded and moved into the passenger's seat. He cleaned the blood from his hands with a petrol-soaked handkerchief and, turning the sports car, drove towards the city.

'It's stupid of me, but I can't remember where you live?'

'Straight through the town.'

The shops were brightly stuffed with Christmas toys and presents; the traffic in the main streets turgid so that he had to wait at each crossing. As they neared the Cathedral he noticed that his companion was trembling violently.

'I say, would you like a drink or something?'

'I – I would rather.'

"Fraid the pubs are closed, it's nearly four, but I've got some stuff in my flat – if you don't mind?'

'I don't mind.'

It was already dusk in the sitting-room as he lit the fire and poured her a whisky and soda. There was a service on in the Cathedral and the strains of an Advent hymn fell in flat sheets of noise upon their ears. She gulped the spirit and then another.

'How do you manage here?'

'I have a woman who does for me. That is, she cleans, makes my bed, sees to my washing, fixes the fire and reads my letters. I get my meals out.'

She lit the cigarette he offered her and began to walk about the long, low room.

'All these books – I'd never have believed it of you.' She glanced at the photographs that stood on the book-shelves. 'And were you abroad?'

'Yes.'

'You know, I'm very vague about you!'

'There's nothing much in my past. Parson's son. Went to a second-rate public school, a place in Surrey for the sons of the clergy. I suppose it's changed now, but when I knew it there was more dirt there than any place I've seen outside Port Said.'

'And then?'

'Out of a job for a bit. The Service – and here. Not very exciting, I'm afraid.'

'Where were you, abroad?'

'Iraq.'

'Tell me about it!'

'Well, the pay's very good out there. I had two polo ponies ...' he stopped as she began to cry.

'It was awful,' she said hysterically, 'it was awful. I saw it.

The noise was horrid. The 'plane just seemed to crumple into the ground. He was screaming when I got there. I hated it. I hated it. The 'plane all flimsy and broken. I knew I hated aeroplanes then. I'll never fly again. It's all grey and lonely. I've always been afraid.'

'Nother drink?'

'This flying was so wonderful. Everyone so happy. You so sweet to me. I'd never been happy before. Not really happy. And now this has broken it. It's like the rest of life. It was awful. I hated it. The noise was horrid –'

'Do you know how we used to cool beer out there?'

'It was awful. The way he moved when I touched him –'

'We used to make a hole in the sand and then put in as many bottles as we wanted. Cover them with sand, then pour petrol over it, which cools the beer by evaporation.'

'I'm sorry, RO.'

'There's nothing to be sorry about, Judy.' She went over to the low window and rested one arm against the top of the jamb, looking out at the Cathedral and the prim, tidy houses that ringed the Close, now all heavily shadowed, hazy with blue mist.

'Doesn't it depress you sometimes? This Close, I mean.'

'No. I like it. It's quiet. And sometimes I go into the Cathedral for a service.'

'I didn't know you were religious!'

'I'm not religious.'

'Robert!'

'M'm?'

'Do you think that when we die –?'

'We go places?'

'Yes.'

'No. I think it will be like sleeping soundly when you don't dream or anything.'

'You aren't – afraid to die?'

'No. If I believed in life after death I would be. But I don't.' She lit another cigarette. 'I can't, Robert, I can't.'

'Can't what?'

'Fly again.'

'Oh, yes you can. Why, everyone feels the same after seeing his first crash. I can remember the time when I was just the same.'

'Can you?'

'Yes,' he lied, and then continued, 'besides, this fellow virtually committed suicide – you heard about him?'

She shook her head, and he told her the story.

'Now, come down to the 'drome tomorrow and I'll take you up for a joy-ride.'

She was silent for a little time. Then he drove her home in the cold twilight and caught a 'bus back to the aerodrome.

3

'That show yesterday shook Judy Hateling up, didn't it?' Janet said as she walked with Robert towards the Tiger Moth.

'Yes. It was very unfortunate that she should have had so much to do with it. Get into the kite and spin her up, will you, please? I want to see Perkins about a dog.'

'OK.'

The GE was doing a daily inspection of one of the Gipsy Moths.

'Good morning, Mr Owen.'

'Good morning. You've heard about the storm that's brewing?'

'What storm would that be?' he banged the palm of his hand on a compression strut.

'About yesterday. Mr Heylead is trying to make trouble about the 'drome not being under proper control. It mostly concerns Mr Hawkings and yourself.'

'I 'adn't 'eard. Thank you, Mr Owen.'

'Not at all. I'm in it too.'

'It's cold this morning!'

'It is. You've been upstairs?'

'Yes. Mr 'Awkings took me up on test.'

When he came out on to the apron again Janet was running up the engine, and the bitter blast of the slip-stream swept dust into his face and blew his sidcot hard on to arms and legs.

He took over control at fifty feet while she pulled the hood up, and then made her climb by instruments to three thousand five hundred. The clouds were high, brushed up into huge towers that reached into the heavens, the oblique rays of winter sunshine giving the silent white hills and valleys a depth of light and shade that intensified their virgin beauty. Sometimes a small patch of cloud would drift towards them, showing a grey, sunless world below as they threaded its cold intimacy. There was snow patchworking the fields on the low hills to the south and the ponds in the quiet farmyards were dull with frost.

Then he told her to fly level and to turn the aircraft through various compass bearings, flying on each for a few minutes.

'Not at all a bad show, though you're still inclined to be set on that rudder and to over-correct with the stick. Now, d'you remember what I taught you about spinning and recovering from spinning by the use of instruments?'

'I think so.'

'What was it?'

'Well, to spin your throttle back and keep her straight with the rudder. When the speed drops to about fifty, full rudder the way you want to go and stick right back.'

'Good. To come out?'

'Put on top rudder, look down at your feet to see if it's on. Then you feel the kite spin t'other way, but don't take any notice. As soon as you've got the rudder on, ease the stick central and forward a couple of inches. The rudder needle goes from four the way you've been spinning to about two and a half on t'other side. Then centralize rudder and when the air speed begins to drop – shove the stick central.'

'Not bad.' He took a good look below. 'Now try a young one, will you?'

The Moth went easily into a spin, was kicked into a spiral by the slots. He bent his head backwards and watched the clouds twisting violently upwards. 'Now,' he cried on the third time round. Janet brought the 'plane out pluckily, but in a few seconds they began to climb until the aircraft was standing on its tail. The sound of the wind in the wires died away. Robert grinned as he waited. His pupil was pedalling at her rudder. 'Look at your pitch indicator! All right, I've got her.' He gave the engine a burst of throttle to keep the airscrew turning and stall turned out.

'That time you were too busy getting the rudder needle central to watch your ASI. Do you follow me?'

'Sure.'

'Otherwise it wasn't too bad. You've got her, carry on climbing. We'll go up and try a couple more.'

When she had done two satisfactory recoveries he asked how she felt.

'I think I'm going to be sick.'

'Shove the umbrella back and have a breather.'

She let the hood flap back and pulled down her goggles.

'God, it's cold!'

'Still feeling sick?'

'N'no. Better now.'

'Right.' He looped and flick half-rolled.

'RO!'

'Yes.'

'You love her very much, don't you?'

'I'm sorry,' he throttled down the engine, 'I can't quite hear you.'

'I said … you love her very much, don't you?'

'You know how much dual instruction costs?'

'Yes. Three and fourpence for every five minutes.'

'Then I suggest that you concentrate on learning to fly and not on my love affairs, or what you consider to be my love affairs. Do a forced landing!'

As she took over he throttled the engine back. She picked a field, got too far down wind, Robert opening the throttle as the hedge came running back at them.

'That may be your idea of a forced landing, but it's not mine, and if you do any like that in your tests you'll be pretty unpopular. It was terrible, a certain crash, enough to make the angels weep. How many times have I told you to pick a field, get down wind, turn up and down always towards your landing ground, judging your drift as you turn. Then overshoot and sideslip the surplus height off when you're sure you can get in?'

'I know, but –'

'And your gliding turns are vile. You must use more opposite rudder coming out. I've told you about it, I've sworn at you, I've shouted till I'm tired. And still you do it.'

'Don't you understand that –'

'Have I given you, "Action in the event of fire"?'

'No.'

'The first thing to do is to turn off the petrol. Then push the throttle wide open and sideslip like hell in an attempt to blow out the flames. If you can, use the hand fire-extinguisher.

When the firing stops, and not before, switch off both mags.
Do you follow me?'

'Yes, but –'

'Pull the umbrella up and do some more head-in-the-bag.'

The Eighth Chapter

1

Two days later a private owner landed his aircraft on a marking board and taxied in without a tailskid.

'What did you find out there?' Hawkings asked Robert when the latter returned.

'Not much. He hit the board for six. Parts of it were scattered over a radius of thirty yards, the uprights were torn out of the ground. Perkins has got that new mechanic busy collecting the bits in a wheelbarrow.'

'Good. By the by, you've heard about the trouble over the supposed lack of supervision when young Limner spun in the other day?'

'Yes.'

'I think it's dying down. Only you might keep your ears pricked up!'

'I will.'

'Oh, I forgot to ask you. How is Mrs Hateling getting over the shock of seeing that crash?'

'She's all right. I took her up for a joy-ride yesterday. She did a spot of dual to-day, and I think she should be able to pass her tests tomorrow if the weather's OK.'

'Right. You're staying for the supper party?'

'Yes. Though I want to go to my flat to change.'

'You can shove off now, there won't be any more flying.'

'Thanks, skipper.'

When he returned to the clubhouse two hours later most of the guests had arrived and were drinking at the bar.

'What ho!' shouted Janet, as he came out of the cloakroom. 'Now you've doffed the motley of aviation, come and knock one back on me!'

'Right!' said Robert, but as he pushed his way towards her, Brown tugged his sleeve.

'RO, old boy?'

'What's the trouble?'

'Will you do something for me?'

'Anything but take those two shop girls back to town.'

'Shop girls?'

'Yes. The two you brought down to watch you fly!'

Brown hiccuped, grinned and turned away.

Janet asked, 'What'll it be?' as they reached the bar.

'A pint, please.'

'Well, down the hatch.'

'Suck in.'

'Busy day?'

'Rather. Over six hours' dual.'

'Tired?'

'Not very.'

'RO?'

'M'm.'

'You know how I shook you up the other day?'

'When I was giving you dual, you mean?'

'Yes.'

'I do.'

'Well, you are in love with her, aren't you?'

'In love with who?'

'Quit stalling – Judy Hateling.'

'You're tight!'

'What's that got to do with it?'

'Nothing. It was just an observation.'

'I asked you a question. Besides, you know by now that liquor only goes to my feet?'

'Yes. I know that.'

'I wish other men did. You wouldn't believe how some

of these social members fill me up with gin in the hope of making me easy to sleep with.'

'You shock me, Janet.'

'And you, no angel?'

'And I, no angel.'

'But you do love her, don't you?'

'Yes,' said Robert, taking her empty glass, 'I love her.'

'Very much?'

'Very much.'

'What are you going to do about it?'

'What the hell's that to you?'

'Nothing. But I'd like to know all the same.' She took her gin and Italian, 'Red on red!'

'Chocks away!' He took a long pull of bitter. 'Well, if it really does interest you, I'm not going to do anything.'

'Strong silent man touch as it were?'

'If you like.'

'But why?'

Robert blew the froth to one side of his tankard. 'Well, because she's married for one thing.'

'What's that got to do with it? He treats her like a dog, from what I've heard.'

'That's just the point. He wouldn't divorce her. He's a self-made man and so's afraid of being laughed at. Besides, he likes treating her like a dog.'

'But he'd divorce her if you did a bunk together?'

'Precisely.'

'Then, why not that?'

'For several reasons. One being that it would hurt my Governor tremendously. Another that we'd be poor, because I couldn't stay on here.'

'You could get work anywhere, you're a split-arse pilot.'

'You want another drink for that, I suppose?'

'M'm.'

'Yes, I probably could, but the Air Ministry might kick up a fuss about my going abroad because I'm still on Reserve.' He collected the drinks.

'Cheers.'

'Cheers.'

'Then, flying isn't altogether a safe sort of job. To begin with, one may break one's neck, in which case she'd have to fend for herself. Then one might be crippled, or not fit enough to pass the doctors or something.'

'You're very much afraid of poverty, aren't you?'

'More than anything in the world. You see, Janet, you've always been, well, comfortably off, so you don't know, you can't know, what poverty means. Rich people tell you there are things which money won't buy, and that's true. But the poor will tell you that there's nothing which poverty won't take away, even to life itself. Love, friendship, happiness, peace of mind, enthusiasm, the desire to go on living, poverty will take 'em all.'

Her voice was suddenly hard. 'I know all about that, Robert.'

'You?'

'All right. Don't look at me like that. I know I'm a little tight. But all the same, you can't tell me anything about being poor.'

'But I thought —'

'You thought I was well-off? Well, I am now, but I haven't always been. My father was a poor parson. He died when I was sixteen. My mother died when I was born. An aunt looked after me for a year after I became an orphan. Then she came off the hook too and left me her fortune. So long as I behave before a lawyer I get a fat allowance. When I'm twenty-one, the money's mine. You'll have another beer?'

'Thanks.'

She got the drinks.

'Here's mud in your eye.'

'Switches off – throttle wide open.' She gulped half her clear spirit. 'I know what poverty is all right. My father was one of those meek, shabby parsons that never get any place. He was weak and awfully ineffectual, always worried, always unwittingly offending people, always afraid of unwittingly offending people, always in debt. We had a lousy housekeeper who robbed him right and left and knocked me about till I was old enough to stand up to her. He'd come up in the world. His father had kept a pub. My mother was county. From what I can gather the only spirit she ever showed was in marrying the Old Man. After that she never got a bean from her people. I think they were very happy, though they were only married for eighteen months. God! I know what it is to be poor.' She lit a cigarette, puffing it nervously alight. 'I've been snubbed in shops as a child 'cause I didn't know we owed large bills in them. Father was for ever filling in forms for charity. Why, we even had clothes from charity. The rich send cast-offs to a society which distributes them to the poor clergy. I was brought up to refer to such clothes as 'things that come'. I went to a good school on a foundationship. They soon found out about the clothes, the bloody housekeeper hadn't cut the former owners' name-tabs out. That took quite a lot of living down.

'I grew to hate money, Robert, but I grew to respect it too. That respect was born in fear, the fear of genteel poverty. I soon grew to learn that money is the greatest thing in life. I used to watch the rich girls at school and hate 'em. I used to think how, if I ever had money, I'd swank and snub the poor. How I'd splash, but take damn good care never to be poor again. I'd rather be dead many times than poor once.

'Through it all my Old Man preached a knock-kneed doctrine of love and fortitude and serving in that state of society into which it has pleased whatever gods there be to call us, brought the art of begging-letter writing to perfection, quarrelled, bickered, argued and fought with the crowd of ignorant bastards that came to his church. But what got me was his attitude to the few rich in the parish. How he worshipped them, went cap-in-hand grinning, became ridiculous in their presence with his obvious fawning. How he stood for the Church and Imperialism and Conservatism in politics. He sometimes used to preach on these subjects, and get into more rows with his parishioners. The trouble was that he hadn't got the brains, or the dignity, or the training, to manage those awful bickerings.'

'Drink?'

'Thanks. A gin, please.'

Now the bar was very full, the intricate fabric of conversation stretching over the rhythmical blare of dance music from the gramophone. He brought the glasses back. Snatches of conversation reached them.

'So every time the chorus high-kicked, we ripped some of the calico …'

'It's quite simple. If the compass needle moves clockwise you push it back with the right foot. If it moves counter clockwise, you use the left. It's called "shoving the needle".'

'They got the kite away on a farm cart. Then this bloke tried to take off. But the grass was very long and he caught his wheels on an iron cattle tank that he hadn't seen.'

'Bung ho!'

'Cheers.'

'I couldn't be that way,' she went on. 'If I couldn't be rich, then I'd be against the rich. No Communist or Bolshevik ever hated them as I did. Then, just as things seemed blackest, he died. He was very much afraid to die. It must be awful to be old and pretending to believe in comforting things. He was very kind to me in his way. After that my aunt took me. And now,' she smiled. 'And now, RO, I do this life well?'

'Very well.'

'For all I care now the poor can go to Hell, if they aren't there already. I'll take good care I never join their ranks again.'

'You're going to make a fortune out of flying, suppose!'

'Don't talk like a sap. I know there's nothing in commercial aviation for a woman except the record-breaking racket, and I don't fancy that. I know I'm tough, but, Christ, I'm not brazen enough for that. I want a 'B' licence 'cause only about half-a-dozen women have 'em. I want it so's people will notice me, as they do now when they hear I'm training. The fools think there's something brave and splendid about a woman flying. They don't realize it takes more guts to bring up a couple of brats on a small income than to fly alone across some ocean or desert. I'm going into this to get my little self into the limelight, and I'm getting what I want. I've plenty of money of my own, or will have soon.'

A steward announced that dinner was served. 'Bottoms up,' said Robert and, having drained their glasses, they joined the crowd that moved towards the dining- room.

2

They taxied in to the tarmac.

'Leave the engine turning,' Robert said. He got out, waved to a mechanic to do up the Sutton harness and the door of the front cockpit and went into the control office. In a few seconds he returned with a small, heavy, glass-topped box.

'Shove this in your pocket.'

'What is it?' asked Judy.

'A barograph – a doings for recording your height. I want you to do five figures of eight round the far wind-sock and the last house in that new row. I showed you how to begin. When you've finished, come in off the last one and do a three-point landing on the circle. You can use the engine coming in if you like. The catch is to do nice turns and to stay put at five hundred feet. Each time you come down the straight before beginning another turn, check your height on the altimeter and if it's wrong, fix it.'

'Five times round?'

'Yes. Five figures of eight and then one for luck. You'll know when you've done five because the steward will put a chair out in front of the clubhouse door, so you won't have to worry too much about the counting. Then if that's all right, you can try the forced landing from two thousand feet, and that done, your 'A' licence is in the bag.'

She took off, made a wide sweep to the north-east and began her figures of eight.

'Nice turns,' commented Hawkings, 'and she's keeping her altitude very well. You've taught her very skilfully, RO.'

'Thanks, skipper.'

He watched the Moth as it floated down the aerodrome, turned, straightened out, floated back and turned again; the note of its engine deepening, softening, deepening, its harsh pulsation boring into his mind as a dentist's drill into a rotten tooth. When he had been up on test a morning mist had held the sunshine till it covered the frost-brittle countryside with a down of gold. But now, it was a cold, sunny day, an easterly breeze holding the wind-socks from their poles and pushing small lumps of cloud across the pale blue sky. There was something impersonal about an aircraft in flight, he thought, that made it difficult to imagine Judy Hateling's frightened concentration as she crouched in the narrow cockpit and sent the 'plane easily about the two marks he had chosen for her.

3

'You know Mrs Alling?' said Bearing at tea. 'You've taken her up for joy-rides!'

'Do I know her?' Robert's tone made Janet laugh.

'At forty-one,' said Janet, 'tut-tut.'

'Is she as old as that?' Brown asked quickly.

'*Et tu Brute*?' murmured Janet.

'Don't be silly.'

'Dear me!' Robert reached for a sandwich.

'What gets me about her', interposed Bearing, 'is the way she leans her body against you when you're scrumming round the bar. It surely shakes one up. By the way, where's young Riseling?'

'Gone up to Town on some secret mission or other,' said Janet, 'and you might spare my finer feelings when you talk about Mrs Alling.'

'You're too intelligent to have any when it comes to that woman.' Bearing turned to Robert. 'That was a good show of Mrs Hateling's, RO, getting her 'A' in such a short time.'

'She had to,' said Brown. 'I hear her keeper's expected home any day now.'

'Know everything, don't you, darling?' said Janet.

'How did the inquest go, RO?' Bearing went on.

'Oh, just as expected.'

'Nothing startling.'

'Nothing startling.'

'Was the kite his?'

'Yes. He'd paid for it, too. I think the joint who sold it to him twigged there was something fishy about it. But cash, after all, is cash.'

'It wasn't insured?'

'What firm would have taken him?'

'He'd cooked it to have the 'plane delivered during the lunch hour?'

'No, I think that was accidental. Apparently he'd been expecting the thing all the morning (one of the ack emmas saw him waiting behind the hangars), but it came just at the right moment. The bloke who brought it down wanted to give him some dual, but Limner told him that Hawkings or I would see to that, so he pushed off to get the midday train. He also told the fellow that he'd learnt to fly in the Reserve.'

'There's something I admire about all that,' said Janet, 'though it surely was a waste of life.'

'I think he was a bloody fool,' Brown said.

'Me too,' Bearing put in.

'I agree with Janet,' said Robert, 'though his determination was probably due to feeling fed-up after being booted out of the Reserve.'

'About Mrs Alling –' Bearing began.

'We've heard all about her,' said Janet.

'My point', Bearing continued, 'is how much misery and trouble is caused in this merry world by this idea of romance that all women have these days. It's indecent, this incredible sense of romance that all women have these days. I suppose they can't help it, living in their bodies as they do.'

'Well, for crying out loud,' screamed Janet, 'as if you were an ascetic!'

'For years', the other answered, 'I've been looking for some nice girl who'd let me sleep with her without all these romantic trappings and baby talk and petting. But can I find one? can I hell?'

'What do you think about all this, RO?' Janet asked.

'I'm an aviator,' Robert said. 'I'm not supposed to think.'

4

He took Judy up for what she called her 'last flip' on the following afternoon. It was a dim winter day and they flew for two hours through the cold, mist-woven air; watching the unreal world, pierced by the glitter of railways, merge into the peaceful sky, while pale rivers and smoke-hooded villages flowed beneath and the clouds echoed to the beat of their engine.

5

When she had settled her bill at the control office, she walked over to him as he stood by the Tiger Moth. He found himself watching her intently, noticing her forehead, puckered over one eye now that she was thinking, noticing the slow, graceful swing of her walk, the feminine dexterity with which she strapped up her handbag. A thousand times he had rebuilt her image in his mind. And yet, he thought, each time he saw her there was something new, some trick of speech, some fleeting expression, that rendered all these mental pictures suddenly jejune, imaginatively lifeless as a photograph looked at too often, or a word repeated until meaningless.

'I've come to say good-bye.' She smiled. 'It's been wonderful, and you've been splendid with a dull pupil.'

'I've been harsh with a very quick pupil. All the pilots I've taught before have been men, so perhaps you'll forgive some of those rows that used to make you sit up so straight.'

'I understand.'

'There's no chance of you – coming down sometimes?'

'I'm afraid not. What I've done already will take enough explaining. Still, it's been wonderful.'

'And you got your 'A'.'

'And I got my 'A'.'

They were awkwardly silent, suddenly tiring of the game.

'Well, you're going on with flying!'

'One gets fed-up at times.'

'Even with flying?'

'Even with being a winged gigolo.'

'That mood doesn't suit you, Robert.'

'I know. Anyhow, good-bye and all the best.'

'Good-bye.' She turned and walked to her car. The wind was rising, rippling the wind-socks, moaning in the telegraph wires. Soon, he thought, it would be laced with snow. He had the propensity, common to airmen, of associating every phase of life with the state of the weather.

The Ninth Chapter

1

'Noticed anything strange about Riseling these last few days?' asked Martin a fortnight later. The school-master was spending his Christmas holidays at the clubhouse, and Robert, who had done only six hours' flying in eleven days owing to fog, was tiring of him.

'Can't say I have.'

'He looks like death. Hasn't been coming in to your lectures either – has he?'

'Now you come to mention it – he hasn't.'

'Wonder what the trouble is?'

'Can't say, I'm sure.'

'Got a woman in a mess, I suppose.'

'Maybe.'

Robert picked up a copy of *Razzle*, but Martin soon began again.

'I see that Mrs Hateling hasn't been down since her husband came home!'

'She hasn't, has she?'

'She won't either if you ask me. I saw them at the rugger dance on Tuesday. You weren't there, were you?'

'No, I wasn't there.'

'Gosh! he was tight.'

'Was he?'

'I should say so. You know, old man, they're a pretty tough crowd – but he went a bit too far, even for them, snatching the trumpeter's trumpet and trying to play it, and barging about and shouting and she looking awfully embarrassed.'

'I've got some work to do,' Robert said. 'See you at tea-time.'

He went slowly through the clubhouse feeling an intense ennui at the thought of being tied for another hour to the familiar rooms in the intimate atmosphere of tobacco, table-games and whispered gossip, the air scorched with central heating. He came upon Riseling sitting on a radiator in the corridor, gazing moodily at the trunks of the petrol pumps that seemed inlaid in the fog.

'Snap out of it! Come and play some table-game or something!'

'I don't feel like playing, thanks.'

'It seems you don't feel like attending my lectures either. I don't want to sound all Oxford Groupish, but you show some more enthusiasm and buck up and do a spot of work, or you'll pip the tests for your 'B' licence.'

'I'm giving up flying, RO!'? In reply to Robert's exclamation he continued. 'You remember how you told me I ought to enlist in the RAF Reserve as a Sergeant Pilot?'

'Yes.'

'I applied, and after filling in a lot of bumf they gave me an interview at the Air Ministry. I got through that all right and then they sent me on for a medical – it's the same medical as the one for the 'B' commercial licence, isn't it?'

'Practically, I believe.'

'By Gad, RO, I'd no idea of what it was going to be like. I knew it was pretty stiff, of course, but Hell's Bells, I didn't expect what I got. All those things you had to do! I mean, blowing into the gas meter and holding up mercury and being spun in a chair and having your blood-pressure taken and eyes tested for about twenty minutes and things rammed in your teeth and up your nose. And having to hold your hands out with the fingers parted and having to stand on one leg with your ruddy eyes closed, and having to hold your breath with a clip on your nose. It took about four hours, and when they'd finished all I could do was to stagger into the Strand and sink a pint.'

'The first board does shake one up a bit.'

'It happens to be my last, too.'

'You mean –?'

'I pipped. Had a letter two days ago saying I was unfit for full flying duties.'

'Was that all they said?'

'Wasn't it enough?' He looked out at the apron where Perkins was starting up his motor-cycle, his jacket turned up about his ears and gleaming with rain. 'I know now that I haven't an earthly of passing the medical for my 'B', so there's nothing ahead and all this money's been spent for nothing. You see, RO, I'm older than I look. I'm twenty-five, and I've made a mess of a couple of jobs as it is. I thought I was going to handle this all right. Of course, flying wasn't as thrilling as I thought it was going to be. You get blasé to what danger there is and otherwise it's very much like anything else. But I did like it, and seemed to be getting on all right. My mater makes me an allowance. When I tell her that I can't get through the medical she'll say that I ought to have thought of that before, and she'll get shirty about all the cash I've blued down here. I suppose one can't blame her really.'

'Why don't you write back and ask 'em if they'll give you another medical?'

'Do you think they would?'

'They sometimes do.'

'But if they did, I'd only fail again!'

'You'd have to get fit. Cut the drinking out, get up early and stay out in the open air. Do gym, play rugger, run, train like hell.'

'I don't think I could go on the wagon now, I've been drinking pretty hard for the past eighteen months. Besides, the others would laugh at me.'

'You worry about yourself and leave the others out of it.'

'You really think I've got a chance?'

'If you do what I tell you – yes.'

And for a week Riseling followed his advice, taking strenuous exercise, drinking only grapefruit, smiling at the jibes and derision of his friends, working zealously at the technical side of his licence. But before ten days had passed, habit proved too strong for him and at first half-apologetically and then defiantly, he dropped the exercises, ignored the opportunity of a second medical board and was back at his place by the bar counter, drinking steadily through the long winter evenings.

2

It grew lighter in the mornings so that the cold electric lights were no longer needed when Perkins began his daily inspection. And with the lengthening of the days, they flew later into the fine evenings, the mechanics as they handled the Moths into the hangars through the dusk, cursing at the thought of June when flying would last for nearly twelve hours a day.

It grew warmer so that morning no longer found the bar windows patterned with ice, nor birds pecking at crumbs by the kitchen door. It grew warmer so that the doughnut wheels of the 'planes no longer scored slow weals through the glitter of hoar-frost on the apron.

Janet Moreton passed her 'B' licence tests, but stayed on at the clubhouse pretending to look for a job.

Spring came to the aerodrome and the lambs who helped their mothers keep down the fresh grass on non-flying days, cried in the late cold. As Robert went up on test he noticed the woods darkening with the advent of the leaves, watched the wind smooth the green crops, saw the streams distorted by spring rain and melted snow till they resembled rivers, and the rivers themselves lie silently over pasture and meadow, the shape of the land preserved by hedgerow and lonely tree.

Riseling failed to pass the medical for his commercial licence and went to live with his mother in Rome. Martin taxied one of the club aircraft into a petrol pump at dusk. The Tiger Moth went away for renewal of C of A.

When summer came the sheep could no longer cope with the grass, the farmers drove hay-cutting machines, brave with red-and-white flags, up and down the aerodrome. (Members soon became familiar with the slow creak of the machine, the jingle of harness, the edgeless words of command; grew to expect the sharp tug at the stick when the wheels of an aircraft taking off caught a ridge of uncut grass.) And now there were more pupils and it seemed to Robert that he was all day in the cockpit, with one pupil as stupid as another. There were landing competitions to be judged and aerobatic displays to be given on Sunday mornings and many rowdy parties that ended in a local county club, where they danced and drank till dawn.

Bearing made a perfect forced landing in a recreation ground while on a cross-country test flight. The workmen took down the scaffolding from the Cathedral tower. Robert spent nine days of his holiday at an RAF Reserve school doing an instructor's course on Avro Cadets as part of his annual training. Then he went home to his father for the remaining week. The river village was gay with summer, the hills above the placid river heaped up through purple shadows. As he caught the early train on the last morning, the sand banks and the south side of the estuary were uniformly grey with morning, seemingly flush with the silver sea, the tiny station that straddled the main line at Ynyslas silhouetted against a roll of mist that pillowed the hills.

They began night flying on two evenings a week.

Groups of tipsy girls would come out of the clubhouse and stand in the cool night, the diffused light gleaming on naked arm and back, while they watched the two rows of yellow flares and the green, red, and white lights of the planes riding through the darkness.

The grass before the apron withered, the wind-socks flapped empty about their poles for many days, parties flew down to the coast to bathe, 'planes had to be left for an hour after tea that the engines might cool.

One of the Air Liners that used the aerodrome flew into a hill in a mist and three passengers and the pilot were burned to death. Robert gave a display of aerobatics at the club garden party which a flying paper described as 'polished'.

It was very hot that summer. The flowers died in the little garden before the clubhouse, the grass burnt up on the aerodrome and on the bank by the petrol pumps which Robert skimmed with his wheels as he glided in from test. The sheep drank from the troughs set out for them, the mornings were hazy with mist. Crowds would gather at the aerodrome gates in the evenings to watch the flying, and Robert and Hawkings would sometimes practise a turn called 'The Instructor and the Pupil', which they were to perform on the afternoon before the club dance. In this demonstration the chief instructor flew perfectly, while Robert, in another 'plane, would imitate him with apparent ham-handed carelessness, falling out of loops, stalling on steep turns, spinning out of rolls, seeming to bounce thirty feet when trying to land.

Two new 'B' licence aspirants arrived. There was a scare when an embryonic pilot, who did not know that it gets dark on the ground when it is still light at two thousand feet, pancaked on the aerodrome in the twilight, wiping the undercarriage off 'JZ'.

The days grew shorter.

3

When the spittle no longer sizzled on the top of the anthracite stove Perkins spat again. Rain nuzzled against the French windows of the bar, rattled in the guttering, in the pipes and gratings.

'Thank Gawd September's 'ere,' said the GE at length. 'I've 'ad enough work this summer to turn my 'air white and I've 'ung round this place till I'm fair fed-up. I don't know 'ow you feels, Mr Owen, but I 'ope it rains all the bloody winter!'

Robert grinned. 'You'd like to spend it by this stove?'

'I would. But I won't. Not with that muckin' Heylead about. I 'ope the next GE they 'as 'ere'll have an Old School Tie or he'll feel lonely, cooped in that ruddy 'angar on wet days. By the way, wot time are we knocking off?'

'Mr Hawkings told me to let you go at five if the weather was bad.'

'Um – twenty-five minutes to go.' He scratched his jaw with the back of his hand. 'The chief's gorn for a medical board 'asn't he?' Robert grunted that this was the case. 'They say that 'e won't get through!' said the GE, looking out on to the aerodrome.

'They said that about his last three boards,' Robert answered, 'but he got through 'em nevertheless.'

The barman came in with a basket of clean glasses and they were silent until he had gone out again. Then Robert remarked, 'I see in the paper that a bloke fell through the bombing trap of a kite at Westchapel yesterday.'

'Killed?'

'Yes. Hadn't his chute on, of course.'

'Careless bastard,' said Perkins. 'How many accidents are due to carelessness, I wonder?'

'Most of 'em,' said Robert.

'Don't often 'ear a pilot say that,' the GE paused, 'though Gawd knows it's true. Was you ever at Westchapel, sir?'

'Not I. Some place, I'm told.'

'Talk about cold!'

'You were there?'

'Yes, on armament. I remember once going up in the back seat with a pilot who was testing a new device for catching empty cartridge cases. 'E was a wonderful pilot, but all of a sudden he says, "This ruddy gun's mucked," he says, and we lands in an emergency landing ground for me to look at it – stopping with the airscrew about touchin' the 'edge. I looks at the gun an' finds an ordinary number two stoppage. Like most officers 'is idea of clearing a gun was to clout it over the butt with a bloody mallet.'

Robert laughed. 'I know all about that. But you must admit that such carelessness doesn't usually risk a crash?'

'Oh, that's nothing. I remember one show after I left the Service, before I worked for these people. I was at a Reserve school. They were flying old training kites in those days. A short pilot gets into a 'plane and takes off without bothering to notice whether he can see over the cockpit side or not. Well, when 'e's at two thousand 'e can't ask for a couple of cushions, so off 'e goes. After a bit he comes in to land, but 'e can't see nothing, gets the breeze up at fifty feet and goes round again. This goes on for some time. On the deck, of course, we twigs wot's up an' gets the blood-wagon and fire-tender out. At last, with petrol runnin' low, 'e decides to 'ave a crack at it and puts the bloody crate through the roof of a garage, settin' the 'ole show on fire. 'E gets out himself without a scratch. A good man would 'ave broken 'is ruddy neck.'

'I've seen shows like that, too. It's very easy to get careless, you know!'

The GE nodded. 'As I looks at it, Mr Owen, there are two danger periods. One is when a pilot's done about fifty hours an' thinks 'e's got flying by the neck –'

'That's the time.'

'An' when 'e's done a couple of years and starts to be split-arse. You know, Mr Owen, half a turn on your raf wires an' shoot-up the girl-friend's house, taking off from the middle of the 'drome and running your wheels along the top of the 'angars?'

'I know.'

'All this besides tellin' the careful pilots where they gets off. Then there's pilots like Mr 'Awkings. They've seen too many good men stall in an' too many split-arse pilots buy it. They takes every precaution and stops club pilots breaking their little necks.'

'The way I look at it is this,' said Robert slowly. 'If you take risks, you most certainly buy it. When you've taken all the care you can, well, as they said in the late unpleasantness, your name's on the one that hits you. I suppose that's the way most pilots look at it, a sort of optimistic fatalism. By the by, you were in the War, weren't you?'

'I was.'

'Ack emma?'

'PBI first, then I did some back-seat gunning.'

'God! I've often wished I'd been old enough.'

'If it's not a rude question, Mr Owen, 'ow old was you?'

'Just three when it began.'

'It's funny to think of you as a war-baby, sir.'

'I suppose it is.'

'Not that there isn't a lot of bull droppings talked about the War, mind you, especially about flying. To 'ear blokes talk, you'd think that everybody 'oo served between '14 and '18 was a ruddy hero. A lot of 'em was, but we 'ad some funny stuff out there, too. The perishing bastards wot stayed at 'ome 'ad the best of it, I reckon. When the next one comes I'm going to wave a flag and pick up some cash. Most of the lot that came out at the end 'ad been shoved into it an' didn't like it. Though, after all, it wasn't so bad.'

'Not so bad?'

'Sometimes it was 'ell with the mud and the shellin'. But you got tough to it. I often wonders 'ow I came out alive. I suppose all the others wonders that too. Not that there's much in bein' an ex-service man these days. People seems sort of sorry for you occasionally, same as if you was a leper or something, but that's all. 'Ave you noticed, Mr Owen, 'ow the ex-service men looks on Armistice parades – shabby an' middle-aged like. Even their medals looks out of place and most of 'em have forgotten wot drill they ever knew. I don't go to those parades now, it seems to me there's something, well, slightly ridiculous about them. Perhaps it's because it's so 'ard to think of 'em as lads going out to France, young and tough, an' fine in khaki, swingin' along be'ind a band. Still, I suppose War is like that. There's something fine about it an' something so bloody cruel it makes you sorry you ain't an animal.'

Perkins spat on to the anthracite stove again as if thus excusing this unusual outburst of verbosity.

'But you're not a pacifist?' Robert asked with a smile.

'Christ, no. Life's all a struggle, anyhow, and everybody's busy bickering with everybody else. Of course, if people 'ad some sense –'

The barman leaned through the bar hatch. 'Mr Owen wanted on the 'phone.'

'Hullo.'

'Hullo, RO. This is Hawkings speaking from the railway station.'

'Oh, you're back in Best?'

'Yes. I want to have a chat with you.'

'OK. Come round to my flat after you've fed?'

'I will. What's the weather like with you?'

'Lousy.'

'OK. Knock off when you like.'

'Thanks. Cheerio, skipper.'

'Cheerio.'

The Tenth Chapter

1

Hawkings looked about the room.

'Nice place you have here, RO!'

'Haven't you been here before?'

'No. It's a snug joint.'

'Suits me. Beer?'

'Thanks,' the chief instructor took the proffered tankard, murmured a toast and began to walk about the room.

'These books and prints –?'

Robert grinned. 'What of them?'

'Only they somehow don't fit you – unless you lead a double life or something.'

'Perhaps I do,' he put his beer on the window-sill. 'What was it you wanted to see me about?'

Hawkings crossed the room and worked his tankard in among the model aeroplanes on the mantelshelf. 'Oh, only that I've finished flying. The medical board pipped me. I'm through.'

Outside, darkness had come down and rain strung the shafts of light that leaned from the windows into the quiet blackness of the Close. Robert could see into the Big School across the way where Martin, in ragged, chalk-ridden gown, was taking preparation, his mouth opening and closing noiselessly as a marionette's when he bawled at the bowed heads, his face flushed in the anaemic gas-light. How the schoolmaster would love this, he thought, would slap the chief instructor heartily on the back as he sympathized with him, would make a stupid speech, studded with witless jokes, at the presentation dinner, would tell all and sundry how he had prophesied this final verdict, had told of its inevitable approach. And because Martin was himself in many ways a failure, he would take that *schadenfreude*, that delight in another's trouble, which is the heritage of oppression and little-mindedness.

'I'm awfully sorry, skipper.'

'Thanks. I'm not going in for self-pity. I've seen this coming for some time.'

'Still, it's pretty tough.'

'Oh, it's not as bad as it might be. I've got a little money – just enough to keep the wolf from the door.'

'You've been luckier than most of us, to have been able to save it.'

'I didn't save it. It was left me by my wife.'

'Your wife?'

'M'm. You didn't know I'd been married, did you?'

'I didn't.'

'One of the few things I kept quiet at the club. Don't breeze it, even now!'

'Not a word.'

'We were married in the last year of the War. It was madness, but everyone was a little mad just then. It was the fashion to snatch at any happiness you saw, not such a bad thing perhaps, as some people think. She died in 'twenty-one at Davos.'

'Tuberculosis?'

'Yes. I watched her cough to death. We were happy for a little while. I suppose we were lucky in that. Some poor sods never get any happiness at all.' He drank deeply and was silent. They listened to the bubbling of the fire and the sweet sighing of the rain outside.

'When – when it was all over, well, life didn't seem worth much. I drank pretty hard. That may be the cause of the trouble I'm in now. I don't know. I wandered about the world.

I flew mails in Canada in the early days there, went on to the States and from there to Mid-Europe. Then to South America, and after that, test-piloting for Gibson's. One place seemed very like another. I used to think I'd never get over it, but time deadens everything. I've been thinking a lot about time lately, RO. I'm not a clever bloke or anything, but it's amazing how one's life slips away, you hardly notice it, the days slipping into years. You sort of always look forward. Then suddenly it's all over and you're looking back. Your life, or the part of it that matters, has slipped away.'

This was a new side to Hawkings and one Robert found difficult to imagine. A still young man, watching the woman who held the very purpose of his life in her continued existence, whose love and interest had helped to thaw a consciousness frozen by war; watching her cough that existence away, her beauty enhanced by the hectic colour which heightened as the disease gained ground. How, in the deadness of that blighted city above the fog-line, in the awful silence of the snow-steeped mountains, he must have been indescribably saddened by her increasing belief in her chances of survival, a belief collateral to the progressive and inevitable rotting of her lungs.

It was difficult to imagine how, when all was over, he had wandered about the earth, seeking to deaden by alcohol that keen stab of rhythmic purposelessness, piercing instantly a mind awakening from the blessed oblivion of sleep or the frowsty darkness of intoxication.

'Nother drink?'

'Thanks. This is rattling good beer, RO!'

'I get a barrel in at a time, but I've got to keep it locked in the bathroom, as the female who does for me thinks it's good beer, too.'

When he had got the drinks Robert kicked the fire into a blaze and they sat on either side of the hearth.

'You've seen something of flying in your time?'

'Yes. I've seen something of flying.' His voice was quiet now, heavy with the dream-coloured scenes that memory was re-building in his mind.

'I remember the first time I ever saw an aeroplane fly. It was over twenty-six years ago. I was a youth then, an articled clerk working for my finals. Flying had always appealed to me, and when I heard that a bloke was going to give a demonstration in a neighbouring town, I wangled the day off. I went by train, I remember. It seems only a few months ago looking back at it. I thought myself the deuce of a dog in a new straw hat and Norfolk jacket. The demonstration was to be given in a park. It was a lovely day and suffragettes were giving away leaflets in the road outside.

'The kite was a Blériot Nine, quite the latest thing at that time, and the fellow in charge had hard work to keep the crowd from tearing it to bits. Most of 'em had never seen an aeroplane before and not more than half-a-dozen had seen one in the air. After a lot of preliminaries (there was a band and the Mayor made a speech) the pilot tried to take off. There was a slight breeze, and he tried to take off down wind. No-one knew anything about taking off into wind in those days. The park wasn't big enough for him to get off and he had to cut his switches to avoid running into the trees that bordered on the road.

'This happened about six times, and then the crowd, who'd paid to come in, began to get restive and jeer. He had a couple more shots and then the police had to help guard the kite and send the people home. Personally I was thrilled stiff, and went over to the pilot, who was a very down-hearted Frenchman. He told me that he'd have another shot on the following day if the weather was favourable. I sent a telegram home to say that I was staying the night, and on the next morning saw the bloke do a couple of circuits round the town.

Then I knew that flying was going to be my job for life.

'You can imagine what my people thought about it. I'd done three years at law and many folks in those days still believed that flying was impossible. I lay mighty low till I was twenty-one and then I came into a little cash of my own. I packed my bag and pushed off for the Blériot Flying School at Pau. I soon learnt to fly, and then things weren't so easy. There were hardly any piloting jobs going, but I kept in with all the fellows in aviation that I knew, picked up some sort of a living in the motor trade and followed Flying Meetings about. Eventually I got one of the first piloting jobs going. Those were certainly the days. The difference between top speed and stalling speed was about a dozen miles an hour, no-one had ever gotten out of a spin intentionally, we flew in raincoats and caps and a cross-country flight usually involved a couple of forced landings.

'Next I did some instructing, and pretty primitive it was in those days. You put your hands on the controls and the pupil put his on top and followed your movements. No dual, no sequence of instruction, no Gosport tubes. You just tried to teach 'em to do circuits on windless days without breaking their necks.'

2

'You've had an adventurous time, anyhow.'

'God, I should say so. Flying's tame these days, though it's still a man's game. But all my time it's been the greatest adventure in the world.' He lit his pipe with easy, certain movements.

'After I'd been on that instructing racket for some time the War broke out. That was the Golden Age. We were making flying history and we knew it. They killed a bloke a day at most training schools, and the majority of the poor blighters who went out to France couldn't fly properly, much less fight in the air. Looking back, one's struck by the amazing acceleration in the evolution of aerial combat that took place in those four years. But when one was in the middle of it, it seemed relatively slow. The War went on for a lifetime. It was never going to end. When one thought of "before the War", it was like thinking of something one had dreamed about.

'I was lucky in the War. I've always been lucky in flying. There's an old saying that there's no good luck in aviation, only bad. It's a saying I've used myself. But nevertheless, I've been bloody lucky. I'm a good pilot, and except for the time I've told you of when I didn't care what happened, I've been very careful. But careful or not, you don't get far without the luck.

'And now I'm done, finished. In a way I'm glad. I've been smelling this for some time. How I know that damn contraption they put on one for blood-pressure test! That warm feeling in the arm, the tingling in the fingers, the saw-bones bloke fiddling with the bulb, watching the mercury as he blows it gently up the tube till you're sick with worry. I've never thought much before about people who aren't fit, apart from feeling vaguely sorry for 'em because they miss so much. I never realized how baffled you are when something beyond your control mucks up your life. You know, RO, invalids have a lot more guts than we give 'em credit for!'

'That's very true.'

'I'm not grumbling, but when one's given the biggest part of one's life to something, it knocks one up to have it taken away. I've seen the aeroplane grow from a dangerous toy to a practicality, from that to the most deadly offensive military weapon ever devised, and lastly blossom into a means of transport and a snobbish sport.'

He paused in his discourse as dreams crowded his mind, gazing disconsolately into the fire. Robert got slowly to his feet and fetched more beer.

'Cheers.'

'All the best.'

'You ought to get my job, but you won't.' Hawkings drank deeply. 'If I know anything, Heylead's bloody brother will duly be installed as chief instructor forthwith.'

'What's he like?'

'I've never seen the sod.'

'Not been in the Service, has he?'

'Not he. I'd clear out if I were you, RO!'

'I would if I were sure of another job.'

'You ought to get one like smoke, the way you fly. The pity is that things are so lousy in flying just now.'

'The only thing for me to do is to hang on and keep my eyes open.'

'If I can put a word in somewhere, I most certainly will.'

'Thanks, skipper.'

'Your skipper no longer, I'm afraid. I phoned Major Yeates to tell him that I've finished at the club.' He drained his beer. 'Gosh! I remember when the club started with the first members sitting on petrol tins.'

Already, Robert thought, he has begun to live in the past. And collateral to the atrophy of his existence, memory, which is another name for the past, will cage his understanding. As he lives and moves in experiences which have gone down the years, the scenes, some remembered with advantages, some emaciated by the passing of time, will be re-created and repeated till his hearers grow weary, and he himself has become a living sham. It will be hard, then, to believe that this man has seen flying develop from an idea into a deadly weapon of offensive warfare, a universal means of transport, that he himself flew through the legendary days, was familiar with those pioneers whose names have passed into the common speech of airmen.

3

'Pity about Hawkings!' Janet said.

Robert looked up from the lecture notes he was preparing. A high wind bumped against the windows of the instructors' room. 'A great pity.'

'What's he going to do?' the girl went on.

'Sell vacuum cleaners.'

'Don't be stupid.'

'That's what most RAF officers do when they leave the Service.'

'I know. But seriously, RO?'

'Oh, he's trying for a ground job, but there aren't many going just now.'

'I've heard a rumour that Heylead's brother is to be shoved into his place.'

'You heard aright.'

'You're not going to stand for that!'

'What do you suggest I do?'

'I dunno. But you're not going to take orders from a little squirt like him?'

'How d'you know he's a little squirt?'

'Must be if he's Heylead's brother.'

'Hardly logic.'

'Damn logic. I wouldn't stand it if I were you.'

'Since you're so interested in my doings, why don't you find me another instructing job?'

'There's no need to be shirty about it.'

'I'm sorry.'

'Don't be sorry. Take me out sometime.'

'I haven't taken you out lately, have I?'

'I should say not. And we used to get along quite nicely.'

'Did we?'

'We certainly did.' She walked over to the window and drummed her fingers on the rain-distorted glass. 'Robert?'

'M'm.'

'You're not still nuts on that Hateling woman, are you?'

'How can you tell?'

'Don't hedge.'

'Well, what if I am?'

'Only that it's bloody ridiculous wasting emotions on dreams when there's plenty of fun waiting.'

'Such as?'

'You don't want me to blush, do you?'

'God! Can you still blush?'

'Then you're not going to take me out?'

'Did I say so?'

'No, but you implied it.'

'Say, rather, that I inferred it.'

'Don't split hairs. If you don't want to, say so.'

'I'll take you out.'

'When?'

'When I've got time.'

'Are you working in the evenings?'

'Yes. I'm writing a book on women who run after men.'

'That's not smart, it's just cheap. You were interested enough in – in all of me – at one time.'

'πάντα ῥεῖ.'

'You're an airman and erudition doesn't suit you.'

'This is the instructors' room and I'm trying to do a spot of work. Scram now, and I'll take you out tomorrow or the day after.'

'I don't want to be taken out as a favour, thank you.'

'Then what the hell do you want?'

'Just to go on as – as we did before.'

'Before what?'

'Before that Hateling woman came in.'

'You leave her out of it.'

'Huh! that's got you on the raw. Don't you fancy yourself, nursing a hopeless passion!'

'I don't know what's the matter to-day,' Robert said. 'You'd better go and take a couple of aspirins or something.'

'All right, I'm going. I know when I'm not wanted.'

'You asked yourself in, remember, and don't slam the door.'

'You men are all the same. Conceited pigs!'

4

In the mornings the cold, grey light flooding his mind, washing away the dark balm of sleep, bringing in the familiar realities of another day. The long drive to the aerodrome, cold engine hissing, the unceasing ripple of tyres on freshly-washed streets. Then test ... *I shall think of this tomorrow, remember how I brought her in for a tarmac landing, holding the wheels a foot above the ground, pulling down the tail, waiting for her to stall into a three-point landing. I shall think of this tomorrow and another day will have passed.*

After that, the long day. Instruction in aerobatics. ('You mustn't throttle back in a stall turn till the nose drops or you may lose your prop.') Instruction in landings. ('You see why you made a mess of that one? Now we'll go round again and try another.')

Hawkings got a job as Airport Manager in the North of England.

Instruction in blind flying. ('You must keep an eye on the pitch indicator when taking off or you're apt to get the nose too high. When I shouted, you were stalled at twenty feet.')

Janet Moreton went on to an Air Line as a publicity stunt, and photographs of her in pilot's uniform were published in the London daily papers.

Instruction in medium and steep turns. In taking off. In forced landings. In map reading. In compass exercises. In night flying. (The regular lights of the city preserving the line of street and park. The friendly glimmer of hamlet, the woods as dark islands, the paler darkness of the sky.)

In the nights: the dark emptiness of sleep.

The Eleventh Chapter

1

'So you have a new chief instructor?' asked Metcalf when he had ordered two beers.

'We have,' Robert answered. The bar of the Ram was filling up as it was twenty minutes to ten. 'We certainly have,' he added as he picked up his tankard.

'All the best. First to-day.'

'Up and down.' The test pilot drank half a pint and then went on, 'I haven't seen him myself.'

'You haven't missed much.'

'Tough, eh?'

'Not so tough. More of a swollen-headed pansy.'

'How does he fly?'

'Not bad.'

'And instruct?'

'As well as you can expect for someone who's never seen the CFS.'

'What's he look like?'

'A wave in his hair and *suéde* shoes with buckles.'

'Oh, he'll be a great success at the club. They don't want a good pilot in that joint; just a social star who'll amuse the women and do the Old School Tie stuff with the men. But, joking apart, it's a crying shame that he's over you!'

'I don't mind so long as he knows his stuff.'

'But, does he?'

'It's too early to tell yet, but I think that being a chief instructor's gone to his head a bit.'

'That's to be expected.'

'He began by putting Perkins and the other ack emmas into a sort of uniform.'

'What did Perkins say to that?'

'Asked if they were to be drilled. Heylead didn't know whether Perkins was laughing at him or not, so had to let it go.'

'How do you get along with him?'

'All right as far as we've gone. When we were introduced he asked if I were Welsh. I said I was. "You don't speak like a Welshman!" he said. "No," said I, "I don't, do I?" What I wanted to tell the bastard was that I knew enough of the inherent social snobbery of the English to profit by the adoption of a golf club accent.'

'And then?'

'It was rather funny. He wanted to find out a lot about the instructing side of the club, but was afraid to ask me a lot of questions lest it weaken his authority.'

'Give him the rope and he'll hang his little self!'

'That's what I'm hoping for.'

They drank in silence. The bar was full to the doors. A fat man with bowler hat pushed back from a red, sweating face led a chorus of banter against the barman, who had bought a string of onions over the counter. He'd paid too much, the fat man said. By God, he grew onions himself. They were his favourite supper with bread and cheese and a pint of mild, and he knew the price of a string when he saw them. Grew onions, did he, the barman replied. When and where, he'd like to know? He was tall, sullenly good-looking in his white coat, very dexterous in pulling drinks.

'You saw Janet's photographs in the papers?' the test pilot began.

'Rather. I hope she's happy now.'

'She's after you, isn't she, RO?'

'She thinks she's in love with me.'

'Gosh! these women!'

'I thought they were your weak spot?'

'They are. A month or so goes by and I begin to worry about 'em. Then I get what I want and hate the sight of females for weeks. Then the same thing happens again. Anyhow, I never met a woman who didn't bore me.'

'If you loved someone?'

'Don't talk about love to me. When one's in our game, as you know, one always has women after one. As long as you treat 'em like dirt, you can get all you want. But if you're stupid enough to fall for 'em, and treat 'em decently, they soon throw you over. Don't I know it? Women can't love, they're too full of romance. By Gad! as if there wasn't enough bother in life without romance!'

'Young Bearing's a disciple of yours, isn't he? I've heard him on the same stunt.'

'We hunt in couples sometimes. By the way, where's he been lately?'

'Oh, on the loose in Town again. He should have got his 'B' about ten months ago, but he's been away for winter sports and fortnights and weekends at Blackpool with that little Jewess from the lingerie shop, so he doesn't get much flying in.'

'Getting tired of flying?'

'M'm, but has to stick to it, as he's gone through several jobs and spent a lot of money.'

'What's the new bloke like?'

'We've got two. Same type. Money to burn.'

'They'll keep on rolling up, till the adventure's taken out of flying.'

Robert raised his tankard. 'May that be a long time.'

2

The firelight dashed small waves of light over him as he sat motionless in the shadows. He gazed fixedly into the fanciful glare of glowing coal, a book, which he had put down as the light drained from a December afternoon, lying open on his knee. The bell-ringers had been practising, the melancholy clatter of changes resounding through the prim Close, beating on his mind in rods of hideous noise.

His sense of ennui and bodily weariness was such that, though his being was jejune of desire, he craved the stimulus of alcohol which would percolate the fog of hopeless futility that clouded his understanding, drive vigour into his tired limbs. But his brain, groping into the future, anticipated with dread the slow levering of his body from the armchair's comfort, the fumbling for switch and the blinding ache of electric light that would strip the room of its shadows, would make it a clean and empty thing, would rob the fire of its magic. Then the quick journey across the carpet, the bite of key turned in lock, the slow hiss of beer running up the polished wall of a tankard.

And what was the future, he thought, but endless days, each as the one before? The frustrations, worries, disappointments, desires and fears that cover present and future, that mount up to form life itself, daily dissolving into the past.

He heard footsteps on the landing, knocking at the door.

'Come in!' The door opened slowly.

'I thought you were taking prep to-night, Martin, or are you breaking up? Anyhow, I'm ruddy glad to see you. Switch the light on and have a drink. I feel like Hell itself.'

'Robert!' she said as light tore darkness from the room.

'Judy!'

'My dear, I had to come. The papers said you were injured.'

'The papers were wrong,' he answered in a low voice.

'You're all right, really all right?' her voice was quiet now, the words tumbling on each other's heels.

'Yes. I'm all right. Feeling a bit depressed, that's all.'

'You did –'

'Yes – I bailed out.' He got up from his chair and looked down at her. Slightly out of breath, flushed by the cold and the effort of running upstairs, she held a small white toy monkey in her gloved hands. Seeing him looking at it intently she smiled. 'I was Christmas shopping. Buying toys. I'd just picked up this when I saw a newspaper poster about the crash. So I put down the money and ran out to get a paper. Then when I read about you being injured, I 'phoned the hospital. But they said they'd heard nothing of you. So I came on here.'

'All I can offer you is beer.'

'Then I'll have a little beer, please.'

He drew her a little in a tumbler and a tankard full for himself.

'Judy?'

'M'm.'

'Why did you come here?'

'I've told you – I was trying to find out whether you'd been hurt!'

'It only makes things harder.'

'What things?'

'Don't be dense, my dear.'

'I'm not dense.'

'You know I love you.'

'You've never said so.'

'You know that I do.'

'Yes, Robert. I know.'

'And you, too?'

'And I, too,' she said.

He walked to the windows and pulled the curtains across. 'Did anyone see you come in?'

'I don't think so.'

'It's very dangerous for you to come here. You mustn't do it again.'

'But we've not –'

'I've never even kissed you.' He smiled. 'The world's a dirty-minded place, my dear.'

'What happened, Robert? It didn't say much in the stop press.'

He waved her to a chair.

'It was this morning. I was testing a secret production of Gibson's. A PV.'

'A what?'

'Means Private Venture. That is, an aircraft which is built on the maker's responsibility, without Government aid. Makers always hope that a PV will prove so successful that the Air Ministry will order it in large numbers for the Service.'

'I see.'

'This particular job is, or I should say was, a light bomber. A monoplane with flaps and a retractable undercart, if that means anything to you?'

'It doesn't – much.'

'Metcalf was supposed to take it up for first test, but he's in bed with flu, so I took it up after I'd finished at the club this morning.

'I got it off all right. I was by myself, of course, with ballast in the back seat. Did some of the usual tests and wasn't too keen on the controls. I wondered if the fuselage was too short to give the necessary leverage. Well, I played about for some time and then did some mild aerobatics. I was giving her the gun to get some speed for a half-roll off the top of a loop when she developed rudder flutter. By the way, don't breeze any of this, it's secret stuff!'

'I'll be as mum as death.'

'I got the wind up and throttled down pretty quickly. Then there was a ripping sound, part of the tail-plane came off and the nose went up for the last time. Then she went into a spin of sorts. I throttled right back and tried to bring her out, but the rudder had gone and so, I believe, had most of the elevators, so I wasn't very successful in that direction.

'Luckily 'd gone up to nine and a half thousand feet before starting any tricks, as you can never be sure of a kite that's straight off the drawing-board. As soon as I found I couldn't get her out, I switched off, shut off the petrol and got the pin out of my Sutton harness. Then I started to climb out of the cockpit.

'There the trouble started. I had a lot of clothes on for one thing as it's a ruddy cold day. The kite was in one of the worst flat spins I've seen, with the nose well up, and I was properly frightened. My foot got caught in something. I can remember screaming all the filthy words I knew and how they were blown away by the wind, for I was standing up by this time. After what seemed an age I got my hands down and cleared it.

'Everything seemed to take a very long time and I had a sense of frustration, like those dreams in which one wants to run from some danger but something holds one back. There's no doubt about danger sharpening one's mind. I remember asking myself what I was afraid of, since I'm not afraid of death. Then I got my hand on the rip-cord ring of my 'chute and got up on the seat. I remembered all the discussions I'd had with blokes about getting out in spins, how they'd all told me that one couldn't get out on the outside. As I leaned inwards, getting ready to go over the side, the centrifugal force threw me clean out.

'I'd never done a drop before and I certainly was frightened. I remembered to wait some time before cracking the 'chute, and seemed to fall for hours. The fear was so awful that it amounted to an ecstasy. I felt something familiar about it, as if I'd been through it all before, as if I'd known it was going to happen all my life. And then quite suddenly I didn't feel worried at all, just very sure of myself.

'I suppose I fell for about four seconds before I pulled the cord. I remember wondering if it felt like that to die – I mean the fear and the sense of familiarity and then the great calm.

'As soon as I pulled the rip-cord, or so it seemed to me, the 'chute opened and gave me the hell of a jerk into a sitting position. It hurt like blazes because I hadn't pulled the harness up tight enough before putting it on. Then I just floated down in perfect silence, looking up at a huge canopy that seemed to distend as the clouds moved over it.

'The kite went down and hit the deck with a roar that I heard some seconds later and then went on fire. By another bit of luck it fell into a field, though there was a village close by.

'I landed in a ploughed field about three hundred yards away and fell forwards, so wasn't hurt. There was only a slight breeze, which meant that I wasn't dragged by the canopy. I gathered it up, took the harness off and went to look at the debris. A crowd ringed it about, all shouting like hell. I bawled at them for a few minutes before I could make 'em understand that there was no-one in it and that they were not, as they thought, having the thrill of seeing someone burnt to death. The mentality of English farm labourers is a standing joke among airmen, but these were cretins. The fire was terrific. I believe they use magnesium in the construction of the engine – anyhow one couldn't look at the flames. They were so bright they hurt one's eyes.

'I tried for a long time to find some bloke who looked sufficiently intelligent to mind what was left when the flames died down, but they were all thick. Next the farmer chappie turned up. He was in the hell of a sweat. I told you it was a turnip field, didn't I? He wasn't so angry about the 'plane as the way the villagers were trampling down his crops. So I was as tactful as I could be. Told him how I'd had to jump for my neck and how lucky it was that the job hadn't fallen on the houses. Then I began to curse the crowd and he joined in, and we managed to drive a good many of 'em away.

'After a bit a bobby turned up on a bike. A fat chap, bone from the neck up, perspiring hard. He took me for a Service pilot, which was useful as he concluded that the aircraft was Government property and started to guard it forthwith. Then there was a lot of saluting and I went off to find a 'phone.

'A crowd of lousy children and all the village idiots for miles around followed me, pawing me when they could as if I were some species of performing animal. They told me about fifty times where the nearest phone was, and at last I reached the place – the local squire's. I left the chorus of morons on the drive and rang the bell. The girl who answered the door thought I was a pedlar, and slammed it in my face. What with oil and mud plastering my sidcot I didn't blame her. I stuck my foot in and asked if I might use the 'phone. She told me to wait, shut the door and went off to find the Great White Chief.

'He was quite a decent bloke who asked me in. I got through to Gibson's while he listened, which was awkward. Everyone's a potential reporter these days. However, I didn't give anything away. Then I put down a bob to cover the call, thanked him for his courtesy and started for the door. He refused to take the money and asked me to lunch. By Gad! Sir! He was the old stamp. So I borrowed slippers, got my kit off and joined the family.

'They'd all got the popular romantic notions about flying, and when the Old Bird had said his piece about my bailing out a few minutes before, the twelve of them started hero-worshipping, which was distinctly embarrassing and made the meal something like the Last Supper.'

'Don't be blasphemous.'

'That lunch was most interesting. You know, feudal stuff still going strong. The squire's missus was a beauty. Tweeds and dogs, soup to the villagers, the local bulwark of the RSPCA. You know the type?'

'I do.'

'The conversation was mostly about huntin'. They'd all been huntin' or were going huntin', I couldn't make out which. I've been in a cavalry mess, and that's somewhere near a mental institution when it comes to intelligence, but this was worse. Every half-minute or so the Old Girl would burst out with "I do think you airmen are brave!" – which made just about enough for one day. I suddenly wanted desperately to explain that the people who're really brave are not the toughs who bail out of aircraft, but those who fight poverty and disease, or those who never get the one chance they want. But I realized that except for education she was on a par with my village friends, so left well alone. Then there was a daughter who was so thrilled that she didn't open her mouth and a scrubby product of our Public School system who asked a lot of damn-fool questions about flying in a voice that hadn't quite broken.'

'What an exciting day!'

'An exciting day, indeed.'

'You're sure you feel all right now?'

'I feel fine. I was depressed when you came, wondering whether I'd done all I could before I jumped. Luckily I saved all my notes. They were strapped to my leg, so I was able to make a full report.'

'You've been up again?'

'Yes. Took a club kite up before tea and did aerobatics.'

'All right?'

'Fine.'

3

'You mustn't come here again,' Robert said.

'But –'

'It only makes things more difficult.'

'Why shouldn't we snatch at a little happiness?'

'Because it would mean poverty. I'd lose my job. And poverty makes short work of love.'

'I know you're right. I'd never have come here under ordinary circumstances.'

'It'll be better, my dear, if you and I don't meet again.'

'That'll be easy.'

'Why?'

'We're going to move to the North of England, though there'll be a flat in London.'

He got up and threw several logs on to the fire. 'Does he – treat you badly?'

'He doesn't mean to. I'm a possession, like his cars, his houses, his social position. A possession he's bought and paid for with brass. A symbol of his ability to get on in the world. Oh, I knew what I was doing when I went into it. I'd had enough of bills and threats. The only thing I didn't know about was you, my dear. However, when the worst comes to the worst, I've plenty of money.'

'His money?'

'His money.'

'Was he angry when he found out about the flying?'

She nodded. 'Another scene in front of the servants, though I'm getting used to them now. I'm getting used to his bragging, his drinking, he's fuddled night after night, to hearing again and again of his brainless success. That a man like my husband can make a fortune is an indictment of English trade.'

'God! if I could only take you away!'

'I've made my bed, Robert, though it's hard lying.'

'Judy! I must ask you something!'

'Anything.'

'Are there other women?'

'I don't think so. He's faithful to me.'

'Judy?'

'M'm.'

'Will you promise me something?'

'Such as?'

'That if – if there were other women, or if anything were to happen to him, you'd let me know. Whenever it might be, wherever you are?'

'Yes, Robert.'

'God knows I didn't want to love you.'

'But you do?'

'I do.'

They spoke no further word till the Cathedral clock struck the hour.

'I must go.'

He kissed her gently on mouth and eyes and then she turned away and went quickly from him.

He picked up the grinning white monkey and set it among the silver aeroplanes on the mantelshelf.

The Twelfth Chapter

1

Robert looked up from his calculations.

'You've worked out your course correctly. Now, off you go.' Bearing picked up helmet and goggles. 'Remember that the secret of a successful cross-country is to fly a good course, keep at the same height, watch the wind and map-read intelligently. All the best.'

'Thanks, RO.'

Robert stretched himself and went over to the window to look at the weather.

'Mastley?'

'Yes, RO,' answered one of the new aspirants for a 'B' licence who was sitting in the bar.

'Get your kit on and start up the Tiger Moth. We'll go up and do some head-in-the-bag.' He tapped the home-made barometer, took his sidcot from behind the door and began to pull it on. The chief instructor came in.

'It's bloody cold up!'

'Yes,' said Robert.

'Oh, there's one thing I want to speak to you about.'

'What's that?' he asked, knowing that the other had been asking each pupil in turn whether he had been kept waiting for a lesson.

'You've been keeping pupils waiting for their lessons lately. One or two of them are getting upset, and we can't afford to lose any flying members, you know!'

He buttoned up his flying suit about his ankles and stood up. His first pupils in the mornings were invariably late, thereby upsetting the time-table till lunch. Also the new schedule drawn up by Heylead made no provision for fetching pupils from the clubhouse, or for getting them in and out of cockpits, which took some time with embryonic pilots in heavy winter clothing. It seemed to Robert to be too much trouble to explain these things.

'Yes.'

'Well, try to remedy it, will you, please?'

He nodded, jerking the chin strap of his helmet tight, and went out on to the tarmac, slamming the door behind him. So it will go on, he thought, this attempting to force a quarrel from every situation, this desire to break my spirit which is born in fear of my popularity, jealousy of my superior training. Each action of mine may provide a cause, each phrase I utter an occasion. For the future any enthusiasm I may show will be snubbed, all my activities will be subtly misinterpreted. I shall turn away wrath with soft answer, cringe to unjust rebuke, bowing my shoulders to unwarranted accusation that I may earn bread. And when I get another instructorship and this farce is over, the desire to snub this bastard which has burned in my mind through many a humiliation will have gone, leaving but a sense of pity and egoistical superiority.

His pupil had started up the engine of the Tiger Moth and was sitting in the cockpit. 'Spin her up!' Robert shouted as he climbed into the front seat. He pulled on his straps, tested the controls, checked the altimeter, watched the revolution counter and oil pressure as the engine roared up, plugged in his telephones.

'Can you hear me?'

'Yes.'

'Taxi her out.'

As the 'plane turned off the apron the mechanic let the wing-tip go before Mastley had waved him away, so that a burst of throttle swung the aircraft dangerously close to a stationary Gipsy Moth.

'Hold that bloody wing!' roared Robert, cutting the master switch. When the airscrew had been swung again the pupil taxied out and took off. It was a cold, raw day and there were clumps of grey clouds above three thousand feet, tall and lonely in the windy sky.

'I've given you "Demonstration of Instruments", haven't I?'

'Yes, RO.'

'OK. Pull the umbrella up, get the seat down, shove the old goggles out of the way. Right?'

'Right.'

'Put your toes on the rudder. Now you've got her, rudder only. Leave the stick to me. Take no notice of what the plane seems to be doing, just keep that rudder needle central on the bank-and-turn indicator. Do you follow me?'

'Yes.'

'Right.'

They flew into a local storm, the rain flung back by the airscrew stinging Robert's face as he crouched behind the small, angular windscreen. He was thinking of something Metcalf had told him on the previous evening. It seemed that the test pilot, who was still in bed with influenza, had succeeded in flattering a society divorcée into putting up the money for a record flight. If the special low-wing monoplane could be built in time, the flight was to take place during Metcalf's annual holiday at the beginning of the following March.

'What the hell's the matter with you? You've got your feet like iron on the rudder! Keep your heels on the cockpit floor and don't over-correct.'

The purpose of this dangerous flight over a great stretch of the Northern Hemisphere was to utilize the resultant publicity as an advertisement for a form of de-icer which Metcalf had patented and with which the machine was to be fitted. But Robert had his doubts concerning the practicability of that de-icer. The test pilot had explained it to him in a restaurant, strangely enthusiastic as he leaned forward in his seat and expounded upon the functioning of his toy with phrases worn smooth by repetition, his voice blaring into the silence as the band finished each item. Almost every aircraft manufacturing firm of repute had rejected it, and should it fail on this flight disaster was almost certain, since they were to seek meteorological conditions ideal for its testing.

'That was quite good. Now, I want you to take the stick alone while I look after the rudder. Again, I don't want you to pay the least attention to what the 'plane seems to be doing. All you have to do is to keep that top needle central.'

As he took the rudder over and settled down to watch his pupil's efforts he was still thinking of the record flight. Metcalf's version of his troubles had nothing to do with the de-icer, but mainly concerned his partner, who expected him to show his appreciation of what she was doing for him by living with her and by taking her with him on the flight itself. The fulfilment of the first condition seriously limited his spare time, while the consummation of the second would deprive him of the services of a co-pilot and navigator. 'Of course, old man, she holds an 'A' licence, but can't be trusted to fly a course, and she's too dull to mug up any navigation. So I'll have to do everything myself.'

Robert had remarked that it was very risky. Metcalf had answered that one didn't get very far in this world without taking chances. Yet, he thought, scanning the sky for sign of other aircraft, one could take too many chances. Test piloting was a good job. It seemed foolish to risk security for the sake of ephemeral fame; to suffer the nervous strain of supervising the construction of the aeroplane and seeing it through C of A, the checking of maps and food supply, the applying for passports and permission to fly over certain foreign countries, arranging for fuel supplies, weather reports, local currency, and working the Press to obtain the fullest possible publicity, for the unlikely justification of an invention.

All through these preparations nothing must be allowed to upset his partner lest she should withdraw her financial support and leave him debtor for work already completed.

Then the start on some windswept Spring morning, the huge 'plane, lousy with mechanics, silhouetted against another day; a few officials, friends and pressmen, all half-stupid with sleep, grouped to leeward of a hangar. Those reporters would have seen many record aspirants climb into cabin or cockpit for the last time, many a disillusioned aviator returning a few hours after starting with engine missing, or beaten by fog, by cloud, by ice, by nerves. But occasionally they would have seen a pilot disappear into the greyness, to spring into fame a few hours later on the far side of the world.

'If you find she's diving and ease the stick back, you must ease it forward again slightly or she'll climb till she stalls. You follow me?'

'Yes, RO.'

Then, he thought, they would be off into the sunrise, each detail of piloting and navigation so carefully realized and rehearsed that the test pilot would be an automaton, flying with unthinking efficiency, trying with an understood uselessness to force the machine onwards by mental effort.

'Now I want you to try stick and rudder together. Hold the stick between thumb and finger only and don't try to fly the machine so much. She'll fly herself very nicely if she's allowed to. Just check any movement of the needles. You follow me?'

'Yes. I follow you.'

The record-breaking 'plane, carrying a weary man and woman whose nerves would be stressed by listening to an engine that for ever seemed to be developing knocks or missing but which would ever be running perfectly, would push its way over mile after mile of Northern Europe till it would seem that they had crossed the whole earth. And at each aerodrome their news value increasing, the crowd would be correspondingly larger, the gradual changing of scene, speech and clothing, uninteresting to minds whose whole purpose would be to get on and on and on till it was finished and they could sleep again.

'Your port wing wasn't down then, you only thought it was. The instruments didn't show it, did they?'

'No.'

'Well, you're supposed to be flying by 'em, you know!'

When perhaps two thousand miles would have been covered, night would swallow them up. Now the tiny cabin (pressed up into the darkness of the sky, where a man forced his sleep-ridden brain to follow compass needle and instruments, his heavy hands to hold vibrating wheel, his racked body to remain upright on heaped air cushions) would be one of the loneliest places in the world. The temptation to fly low over a spattering of lights that marked some Asiatic town, to catch a glimpse of mundane things again after hours during which there had been no sight of wing, of sky, of earth, would be wellnigh irresistible. Then there would be the temptation to turn back to towns which he would know had airports with night flying equipment while only wild country and bad weather lay ahead.

All this time there might be failure of petrol, oil pressure or ignition systems. The engine might run a big-end or break a con rod. The variable-pitch propeller might go to pieces and wreck the 'plane. They might lose their way and fly into some hillside or be beaten down by storms. Ice might form on aerofoil or airscrew.

Centimetres of ice, freezing with a rapidity which would give no chance to Metcalf's invention, altering the essential shape of the wings so that the aircraft would stagger earthwards, the pilot powerless, his mind hardened against inevitable disaster. And when morning caught them up again, Asiatic peasants would find them as they went to the fields, at peace among the debris, the woman who had sold her life for lust and sensation, the man who had given his skill, his existence, for a useless toy. To these simple people whose life was work and sleep, these two would represent a divinity, would belong to a world where there was security and food and shelter, where life was not one weary, cyclic fight that made death at least not a thing to be despised.

Then the news of the disaster, travelling by slow stages to the nearest telegraph, would suddenly be flashed about the world, to scream from a thousand newspapers. But in a few days it would be forgotten again save by one or two persons who would weep in self-pity for something, in the death of another, which had died in themselves.

2

When his pupil had flown for another ten minutes Robert ordered him to push the hood back and to take a breather. Then they began once more. This time he was taught climbing and gliding. The front cockpit instruments were steamed up by the change in temperature, and Robert had to beat the numbness out of each hand in turn. After they had glided down to two thousand four hundred he began to fly level. Leaning forward to shout some corrections through the telephones Robert suddenly saw a black Avro Cadet approaching head on, rocking on its wings as it hit a bad bump.

'I've got her.' He pulled the controls from his pupil and slammed the aircraft into a steep right-hand turn.

At the same instant the other pilot saw him and turned to his right, so that the two 'planes, which had been in some danger of collision, passed with fifty yards between them. Seeing the hood over the Tiger Moth's rear cockpit the other pilot raised his hand behind his windscreen, smiling with a flash of even teeth that made his goggled face temporarily human. Robert raised his hand in return and then they had passed and were each out of the sight of the other. He wondered whether they would come across one another again, the two who had met for an instant in the clouds, grown familiar in the exchange of a common courtesy.

He leaned forward and spoke to his pupil.

'You've got her. Carry on flying level on a bearing of a hundred and eighty-three.'

3

'What's the book?' Robert asked as he pulled off his helmet. Mrs Alling held up her novel that he might read the title, smiling at him over the dust-wrapper.

'Beverley Nichols' *Self.* Have you read it?'

'Yes. I've read it,' Robert said.

'Did you like it?'

'Yes. I thought it one of the greatest novels in the world.'

'Really?'

'Really. A work of genius. Worthy to stand with *Crime and Punishment*, *To the Lighthouse*, *Bovary* and *The Magic Mountain.*'

'Now, I've a teeny, weeny suspicion you're making fun of me?'

'Oh, no, Mrs Alling, instructors never make fun of their pupils.'

'I'm not so sure of that.'

It was difficult to believe that this was the woman he had heard snarling at her husband a few days before when the latter had been a few minutes late for dinner. She had continued to treat her spouse with bad-tempered indifference throughout the ensuing meal while Robert struggled to keep some sort of conversation alive. But then, he reflected, glancing at his wrist watch, this man was only her husband, only worked all day to earn money for her to waste. Men had been doing these things for her all her life, she had grown to expect such actions, believing them to be a tribute to her wit and beauty.

At the moment she was undoubtedly interested in what she would have called romance.

'Is it time for my lesson?'

'Yes. If you're ready we'll go out and do battle.'

He helped her on with her leather coat.

'It's most awfully intriguing to be learning to fly. I never thought I'd screw up enough courage to begin.'

'Well, you did.'

'I'm afraid I'm not as clever as your other woman pupil, Mrs Hateling, was.'

'The quickest pupils don't always make the best pilots,' he answered mechanically, wondering whether this mention of his late pupil was altogether accidental.

She paused on the apron in the shadow of 'EW'. 'My helmet strap,' she laughed apologetically, 'would you do it for me, please?'

Realizing that she wanted him to touch her he eased a slight crease from the leather thong and tightened it beneath her chin. Christ! he thought, I've certainly got a man's job in the world. But once they were taxying he remembered only that he was teaching a stupid pupil to fly.

'As you taxi down wind, put the stick right forward so that the wind, blowing on the down-turned elevators, will help to hold the tail down. Do you follow me?'

'Yes, RO.'

She fumbled with the controls for some seconds, trying to turn the machine dead into wind, then played about with the cheese-cutter till Robert set it for her. He hated taking off in the direction in which they were facing as it involved not only using the shortest run on the aerodrome but also a forced landing among the shambles of a new building estate should the engine cut out during the first few hundred feet.

'Is it all right for me to begin?'

'Wait till this 'plane's landed, then you can go.' The 'plane in question was the Tiger Moth containing Martin, who, seeing Mrs Alling put the stick forward till 'EW's airscrew clipped the grass as she took off, raised both hands in mock horror. Robert grinned in reply. The Moth staggered into the air about half-way across, Robert pointing upwards so that Mrs Alling should climb more steeply.

At a hundred and fifty feet the engine coughed, spluttered, picked up again and then cut.

'I've got her.' He rammed the nose down hard, leaning sideways in his cockpit seeking some sort of landing ground amongst the half-built houses. He was horribly frightened, very cool, very certain of himself. There was a causeway of railway sleepers running between two rows of half-built houses upon which a Gipsy Moth might conceivably be landed, though to reach this rough roadway he would have to turn through at least sixty degrees.

Without hesitation he slammed the Moth into a steep turn, pulling out with the nose on his objective as she stalled. Down went the nose again till the wires sang. As he waited for drift to become apparent, for this would be a cross-wind landing, he became aware of his pupil, who was screaming something about a crash and clutching the stick so that he had to use both hands to keep it forward. He laughed through the telephones. 'There isn't going to be a crash – let the stick go and pull the pin out of your harness.' To his relief the tension on the stick was suddenly eased, and with free left hand he cut the master switch, brought the cheese-cutter right back, turned off the petrol, closed the throttle and undid his harness.

He skid-slipped a few feet off and, straightening up, put a wing into the drift. Ten seconds later he dropped the 'plane for a perfect landing, the tail-skid rattling on the uneven sleepers. He kicked on rudder to turn down wind and the Moth bumped to rest, the airscrew within ten yards of a slovenly fence. As he swung himself to the ground he took a deep breath and let it out very slowly. The Moth was undamaged and his pupil had fainted. He caught her by the collar and pulled her face out of the compass, wondering whether she would continue her flying lessons. It was unlikely, he thought, letting her limp body slump back into the cockpit when he was certain that she was uninjured. She had wanted to learn to fly because it was romantic, because flying was expensive and therefore fashionable, because flying was generally believed to be dangerous.

That she should be braving this danger appealed to her, enhanced her standing amongst her acquaintances and (as she was devoid of imagination and was consequently unable to visualize anything resembling a crash) gave her a sense of innate confidence. Now that she had been in something approaching danger and as she was certain to be told that had Robert attempted to turn back to the aerodrome (as she would have done if flying alone) she would have been burnt to death, flying would immediately become distasteful to her and the club would lose a wealthy pupil.

He could hear shouting, see a crowd running up and the figures of the aerodrome staff silhouetted against the horizon as they climbed the boundary fence. He turned and looked at the Gipsy Moth, stretching out a hand to touch the ribs that protruded through the doped fabric as bones in a consumptive's hand. So this aircraft, standing neatly among piles of bricks and sand, surrounded by planks, concrete mixers and half-built houses, was the climax of his flying career. For that perfect landing in exceptionally difficult circumstances he had given years of his life, struggled through the drudgery of many a ground course, passed stiff medical examinations, endured insults, had enthusiasm derided, had taken countless precautions, had built and rebuilt the fabric of expected danger in his mind till each feature had become familiar, a thing known and understood.

And now he was thinking of the work to be done. How Mrs Alling would have to be attended to, the building contractor pacified, the fence pulled down, boards laid on the mud, the crowds held back, the police asked into the club for a drink, the wings of the aircraft folded and the wheels greased. He began to laugh, imagining the disappointment of reporters when they discovered that no damage had been done, the chief instructor's chagrin at having to congratulate him before the club members.

Now the first of the aerodrome staff was a few yards away, his face stupid with anxiety.

The Thirteenth Chapter

1

The village now, he thought, would be quiet with winter, sand drifting noiselessly, incessantly on to the roadway, collecting in gutters, piling in ridged sheets to westwards of steps that led to shop or empty boarding house, sand that was swept away daily and tipped on to the shingle opposite the tall, bleak church. When the wind was easterly it would ruffle the incoming tide, dry the sandbanks in the estuary till they were hazy with driven sand, blow coldly off the river, causing the stevedores to beat their numbed hands together as they unloaded cement from dingy tramp steamers.

Mrs Alling decided that she would never fly again.

Occasionally the hills on the southern side of the estuary would be sharp with snow and fishermen would work through the bitter, still weather, raking mussels from the river bed, empty sacks slung over their oilskins.

Metcalf and his companion were killed when their record-breaking monoplane flew into a hillside in Western China.

When a gale sprang up and scud littered the shore, the waves would slap on to the promenade at high-tide, wash over the roadway and flood the cellars. Girls, giggling as they waddled arm in arm, would dodge the hissing spray. Fishermen, the light from street lamps splashing on their wet oilskins, would crouch in sheltered corners, watching boat and low-lying storehouse till the tide should go down and the danger would be past.

2

'So you've had a row with the chief instructor?' Martin said as Robert pulled up his car outside the Cathedral School gates.

'I have.'

'I was in the bar at the time. We could hear everything he said, but you were inaudible.'

'Good thing perhaps.'

'You let him have it?'

'I did.'

'What's he doing about it?'

'Trying to get me kicked out.'

'Any luck?'

'Not he. Majority of the Committee voted that I stay on.'

'I'm glad.' The schoolmaster switched on the dashboard light and looked at the time. 'He's a bastard,' he added with sudden venom.

'He flies well!'

'You're better.'

'More experience.'

'Well, he's a bloody instructor anyway!'

'You hate him, don't you?'

'I've reason to.' There was a pause and then he went on, 'I'm supposed to be on duty to-night, but it only means being on the premises as there's a lantern lecture instead of prep. Come up to my study and have a bottle of beer?'

'Thanks, I'd love to. Give me a minute or two to shove the 'bus away!'

'Right, old man, I'll go on. See you inside.'

Five minutes later the schoolmaster came upon Robert in the main corridor surrounded by a crowd of small boys who clamoured for his autograph.

'You're quite a hero to these kids since you bailed out of that monoplane.'

'I hope the average hero's reputation is founded on finer deeds than the saving of his neck at any price.'

Martin laughed and led him up a worn, metal-shod staircase to his study. It was a large, dusty room, lit by a shadeless bulb and warmed by a tiny electric fire. A large curtain was drawn across one end, hiding the schoolmaster's sleeping quarters. On the walls were photographs of Oxford societies, two enlargements of groups taken at the aeroplane club and a small tin shield painted with the arms of BNC. A ragged gown, grey with chalk dust, hung behind the door in company with a flying helmet, a cane, a sidcot, and a bag of golf clubs.

On one side of the room was a bookcase stuffed with text-books and detective novels, while a case of bottled beer which stood beneath the windows was partly camouflaged by muddy games' clothes. The only other furniture consisted of two armchairs and a kitchen table piled with exercise books, each folded within the next.

''Fraid I don't live in style like you.'

'What's the matter with it?' asked the instructor, sliding into one of the armchairs. His companion grunted as he opened half-a-dozen bottles of beer.

'It's not as I'd like it to be. You see, I have to help my people financially.' He disappeared behind the curtain and returned with two glasses. When he spoke again his voice, it seemed to Robert, was too casual to be carrying spontaneous thought, his scrutiny of the beer too thorough to be more than a mask for agitation.

'Has Heylead, the instructor I mean, told you anything about my people?'

'No,' Robert lied.

He brought the beer over.

'Thanks. Cheers.'

'Cheers.'

'Have you heard that he's said anything to anyone about 'em?'

'No,' lied Robert again, and took a deep draught. The beer was very cold.

'Well, he's been breezing a lot about the club. He's had his knife into me from the very start, must have heard me jeering at his instructing or something.' Martin put his beer on the floor and turned the electric fire on fully. 'You know that ginger-headed little whore he's running round with?'

'Surely.'

'She's from my home town. As soon as she saw me, she recognized me. Then I knew that he'd have a handle he wouldn't hesitate to use. You see, RO, my father's a butcher!'

'Is he a good butcher?'

'Yes – yes, of course.'

'Then what of it?'

'You know. They're not all like you at the club. Flying clubs are the most snobby places in England. I was only just holding my own before. Now he's putting it about that a sister of mine used to work in Woolworths. It's true. That's going to help things, isn't it?'

'You worry too much,' said Robert, standing up and walking over to the window. 'You're not unpopular at the club!'

'I'm not popular either, and you know it. I've wanted to be popular all my life, but people never seem to really like me. I've been handicapped for one thing. I won scholarships to the local Grammar School when I was a kid. I'm not really brainy, so I had to work like hell. I wasn't good at games either, so I was thoroughly cut and considered an outsider.

'From there I got scholarships to BNC, but not enough to cover everything, so my people mortgaged the business to help me through. I've paid most of that off now, but it will be another year before I'm clear. When I was up at Oxford I couldn't afford to splash and I had to work like the deuce to be sure of getting a second. I never got in with any of the best people. I wasn't exactly unpopular, but if I'd gone out and hadn't come back, no-one would have missed me.

'Even now at the club I've got to be fairly mean because flying's so expensive and I'm still paying off that mortgage. So you see I've never had the leisure and the money to get in with people. I often wonder if I'd be a damn sight happier serving in the shop with all my dreams unrealized.

'Again, I can't carry off my position properly. My manners are too good, like the table manners in Lyons Corner Houses, and when I try the free-and-easy stuff, it just doesn't come off. I suppose I'm too self-conscious, too eager to please.'

Robert looked down at the boys, who were filing across the yard on their way to the lantern lecture. They passed lifelessly through a strip of light that fell from a barred window. Dressed in shabby, black clothes, the shoulders of their jackets were powdered with scurf. The juniors wore their Eton collars out of sight; every boy dragged his feet in heavy boots. Many of them were appallingly ugly, while a few looked decidedly vicious. A pimply prefect, who had grown out of his trousers, yelled in a thin pseudo-Oxford accent that the lecture was due to begin and that the last boy would get fifty lines.

He turned to Martin, who leaned against the mantelshelf. 'You make too much of it all. Everyone in the club has come up in the world, or their parents before them. Besides, they don't mean to be snobs. Snobbery is a beastly characteristic of the English, who're otherwise very nice people. Just be yourself. If you don't bother about how you impress those you meet, everything will be fine.'

'I wish I could. But I can't do the things you do. I always feel irresistibly drawn towards people with money or position. It's a form of ambition, I suppose. And yet, when I meet them, I can't be sure of myself. And I'm just as snobby as they are, in my way. The trouble I take to keep my relations away from this place!'

'Oh, I understand that. It's because of the boys. They're thoughtless, cruel little swine at the best. Look here, Martin, you're brooding over this too much. These are democratic days, and apart from that, you ought to be proud of having come up in the world.'

'The trouble is, I want to be a gentleman, and that's just what I never will be.'

'A gentleman is a bloke who never seduces a girl of his own class. Drink up your beer and don't worry.'

'I have been worrying rather a lot.'

'I should think you have.'

3

There was a burst of cheering from the lantern lecture. Robert finished his beer.

'’Nother?'

'Thanks.'

'Any chance of you getting Metcalf's job, RO?'

'No. Heylead senior's one of the directors of Gibson's.'

'I'd forgotten that. Incidentally, have you heard any more about that crash?'

'Metcalf's people had a report from a German pilot who's flying on some Chinese airline.' He took his beer. 'Thanks. Cheers!'

'Cheers!'

'This German says that they were very much south of their course. He thinks they were forced southwards by a gale and that, coming down to get a fix, they flew into a hill.'

'He was a nice bloke.'

'Yes. I've missed him.'

'Silly ass to try that flight, though!'

'Maybe.'

'Pity there's no chance of you getting his job, RO!'

'I'm hoping to get into a Reserve school one of these days, only keep it under your hat.'

'I will.'

'Then I'll get more time off and the pay'll be better.'

'Talking about money,' said the schoolmaster. as he poured himself another glass of beer, 'I'll bet Hateling left a tidy pile.'

Robert's heart kicked.

'Hateling?'

'Yes. Though he'd probably fixed the death duties before he came off the hook. You know how cunning these millionaires are when it's anything to do with cash. Their wills never really tell what they've left.'

'Hateling's dead?'

'Rotting by this time. About two months ago, should say. Didn't you see it in the papers?'

'No – no, I didn't see it. What did he die of?'

'Pneumonia, poor sod!' Martin drank half a glass of beer. 'Oh, he did quite well. Fine obituary in *The Times*. Reading it, you'd think he was some use in the world. Have another drink?'

'Thanks.'

'I wonder if we shall see Mrs Hateling at the club again?'

'I wonder.'

'I bet she was glad to see him going!'

'Yes.'

'Well, here we go again. Cheers!'

'Cheers!'

4

He ruddered the compass needle on to red as he came out of the last climbing turn so that he was on his course as he flew over the aerodrome. It was a cold, clear morning and the Tiger Moth rocked in the bumps as he crossed the low hills to the north-east of the town. To be flying alone made him extremely happy, and he sang softly as he looked down at the conglomeration of houses lying at the base of a great tower of smoke that leaned drunkenly into the clean emptiness of the sky.

As I fly, he thought, my speed robs the world of motion; the noise of engine, airscrew, wind in the wires, absorbs its many sounds. As I journey eastwards my mind, in common with all airmen, soars above the world. As I journey with the wind for a cloak and the clouds far beneath my feet, I rise above the frustration that is life, above strife and jealousy and hatred; above money, above ambition, above desire. And even the steam of a train, creeping into the still countryside as ink soaking into blotting-paper, cannot convince me of the enveloping futility of mundane existence. Even the knowledge that men have twisted flying itself into an instrument of murder cannot deny me a state, politic and continent, cannot prevent me finding a great stillness of spirit in this lofty contemplation of the trivialities of my understanding.

The Fourteenth Chapter

1

He noticed that the interior decoration of the flat harmonized with the Van Gogh prints that were hanging in hall and lounge. The traffic in the Edgware Road murmured everlastingly, and remembering how the east wind had swung into his face at every corner, he moved from the steel-framed windows to the electric fire. It was a pleasant room, starkly furnished in the modern fashion. In the paper rack were many copies of *Flight* and *The Aeroplane*, while a number of books on learning to fly seemed primly out of place among the poetry and modern novels that lined the long bookshelves.

Judy came in.

'Robert! I'm awfully glad to see you. How did you come up?'

'Blew. Brought the Tiger Moth up to Hatfield for renewal of C of A.'

'What was it like flying to-day?'

'Cold and bumpy.'

'Do sit down. Tea'll be in in a minute.'

'It's good to see you again, Judy.'

'Is it?'

'Rather.' He picked up a tiny reproduction of a Borzoi single-seat fighter modelled in silver that stood on the flat arm of his chair. 'I've been admiring this!'

'Have you done much testing lately?'

'Yes, I've been pretty busy. Spinning tests with a new type.'

'I hope you're more careful than you used to be!'

'I don't have to be now. I've a mascot.'

'And what may that be?'

'A toy white monkey.'

He lit her cigarette.

'Judy!' he said when she made no reply, 'as I told you on the 'phone, I hadn't heard about your – trouble – till Martin blurted it out last night in the middle of a conversation about social ambition.'

'How is the Ground Instructor?'

'Just the same. Judy! you won't think me a hypocrite if I say I'm sorry?'

'Of course not, my dear. I understand.'

He got to his feet and stood with his back to the fire.

'So you're free at last?'

'Yes, I'm free.'

'Happy?'

'Not as I thought I'd be.'

'You promised you'd let me know, Judy, if anything happened?'

'I did.'

'But you didn't let me know, did you?'

'I was afraid that perhaps you were in love with an ideal you knew you couldn't attain, and that knowing you couldn't attain it, you loved it all the more.'

'I was afraid too. I wondered if you'd despise me for not having taken you – for not having grabbed at what little happiness was in sight.'

She tilted back her head and blew a little cloud of cigarette smoke towards the ceiling. "The Man who respects Woman shall be despised by Woman", is that what you mean, Robert?'

'Blake?'

'M'm.'

'I was looking at your books before you came in. We have vices in common. Good grounds for marriage. You'll marry me, won't you, Judy?'

'You said you were afraid?'

'Not since I've seen you again. As soon as you came in I knew I loved you.'

'You did, did you?'

'You'll marry me, won't you?'

'Yes, Robert.'

'I only want your money, you know!'

'I realize that.'

'When?'

'Eighteen months.'

'Why so long?'

'Convention. You'll have to be scrubbed and taken to see my people.'

'What are they like?'

'Galsworthyish.'

'You'll drive me crazy, keeping me waiting eighteen months!'

'Don't be stupid.'

They were silent as the maid brought in tea. Then Judy began to pour out, the silver teapot flashing with the last of the light, Robert finding a strange satisfaction in his contemplation of her certain, dexterous movements.

'How are things at the club?'

'Much the same. Bearing's got his ticket at last and's flying on the Irish ferry as second pilot. Janet had a job on East English Airways, but they went bang. The last I heard was that she was in Germany. Of course, you heard about Metcalf?'

'There wasn't much else in the papers for days.'

'Poor Metcalf, he got his publicity all right.'

'You were good friends?'

'Yes – still, that's the way he'd have chosen to die.'

Flying was like that, she said, like war which took the best. There was a hardness in her voice that was new to him.

'You know that Hawkings has finished instructing and now looks after an airport?'

'M'm. That was before we left Best. I never thought then that I'd be living there again.'

'You won't, my dear.'

'But –?'

'I won't be at the club much longer. There's a better job in view at one or other of the Reserve schools. The pay'll be about twelve quid a week, so we'll be quite well off!'

'There's no need to worry about money, Robert. I've got so much that it frightens me.'

'Save it to educate the children. Send 'em to the best schools and they'll grow up to join flying clubs and sneer at their father because he earns a living!'

'They'll be the dullest children, Robert!'

'And consequently not unhappy.'

'There'll be Bertha, she'll ride well. Good leg for jodhpurs.'

'Tweeds, big feet, dogs barking in the stables.'

'And Edward?'

'Debts at Oxford. Shop girls. Thick-headed but sweet to his mother. Good pilot in the Auxiliary, bawling at his back-seat man not to treat him like a taxi-driver during bombing practice.'

'What about Mary?'

'Ah! she's the intellectual one. Reads James Joyce at six. Saves her father from drink. Dies at eight hearing the flapping of angels' wings. You see how flying comes into my life at every point?'

'I'm coming down to Best before you leave. I want some dual in blind flying and aerobatics.'

'I'll let you know when the Tiger Moth's ready. It'll only be a week or two. Then you can really begin to learn to fly.'

While chatting with the AID man who had driven him into London from Hatfield, and as he walked from the Edgware Road into St John's Wood, he had been conscious of a dread-filled ennui at the thought of meeting Judy again. So often had he dreamed the scene, so many times had each detail fitted into its place in his mind, so surely had his imagination gone before him, that he had feared its subsequent enacting as being empty of all but a recital of brittle phrases masking changed emotional standpoints. But now, as he watched her in the wilting light of a March afternoon, the glow of the electric fire emphasizing the lithe, firm line of shoulder, breast and thigh beneath her tightly-fitting black frock, as her words, her movements, her gestures fell easily into their places in his understanding, he felt a sense of tenderness, remote from physical desire, that was new in his relationship with a woman.

2

'Who's the new chief instructor?'

'Heylead's young brother.'

'Is he good?'

'Not bad.'

'You get on well?'

''Fraid not. He hasn't been in the Service, but did an instructor's course at some flying school. This weakens his authority and naturally makes him jealous of me. There was trouble from the very start. I knuckled under because I like peace and didn't especially want to lose my job. Being an Englishman he took meekness to mean weakness and began to bully. Then we had a good row and now he wants to be friendly again. I can't live that way, Judy. If I have to have a row, that's all there is to it. A quarrel with me is the finish, not an initial testing of strength.'

'You don't like the English, do you?'

'As a race, I admire 'em.'

'It's hard to reconcile such views with the Robert who used to lean on to the shoulder straps and bawl caustic instructions through the telephones!'

'I hope you haven't forgotten all I taught you.'

'Rather not. I've gone over it many times.'

The maid cleared away the tea things. Judy pulled the curtains over the naked windows and turned on the reading lamp.

'Robert!'

3

The train swayed as it rode through the points. A framework of signals loomed above, the lights twinkling with easy precision from red to green. In the windows of the villas that backed on to the line Robert caught intimate, fleeting glances of other people's homes, of maids drawing curtains, women stooping over sleeping children, men turning on the wireless, each picture sharp and clear-cut, without movement, as a tiny photograph stuck on to the blackness of the night. To the north and east and south, he thought, lay the thousands of such houses that go to make up the greatest city in the world; the street lighting stitching the many roads and avenues into seeming symmetry. Human experience was common to all these homes, and yet to each individual life came afresh, untasted, a thing wonderful in its interests, fierce in lust and fear, tender and overwhelming in beauty.

And as a man lived, pitting his courage against frustration and poverty and disease, as death ended the lonely journey and the farce was over, it would seem that his joy had been all the joy of the world, that no suffering was comparable to his suffering, that in his dying the world too would perish.

The train bored its way through the darkness, light from the rigid windows rippling in two broad streams on either side of the track. Opposite Robert sat a sickly youth in shorts and khaki shirt who nursed a bulging rucksack. Between his bony knees stood a heavy walking-stick, his brogues were clumsy with nails. A girl, similarly attired, sat by his side and they talked in frightened whispers, the cadence of their flaccid phrases intermingling with the clatter of the train. From time to time the youth would look beseechingly at him, then flush and turn away.

He thought of the time when his own life had been encircled by shyness, when every action and every word had needed an effort of will, when each strange meeting had been a test of courage. He remembered how anticipation had been loaded with fear, memory heavy with doubt. Now that he had the confidence in himself that arose from indifference to the opinions of his fellow-men, he could afford to smile at what had once been an agony of mind.

There was some frenzied whispering on the opposite seat and then silence. The girl nudged her companion, who swallowed and asked if Robert would mind the window being lowered. It was very hot in the compartment, he added with eyes downcast.

'If we change places,' Robert answered, 'you can do what you like with the window. I'm not very fond of fresh air myself.' When he had settled down with his back to the engine he turned up the fur collar of his flying coat and thrust his hands deep into his pockets.

'Don't you think plenty of fresh air is essential to keep fit?' asked the girl in a genteel voice.

'I do. But in the proper place. And the proper place to me is outside.' They were silent and he went on to point out that those who live open-air lives – farmers, sailors, airmen – are usually the first to shut windows. The clerk disagreed with this, and they began a discussion which was interrupted by Mastley, who came in from the corridor.

'Hullo, RO! Been on the razzle?'

'I'm too old for that sort of thing. What are you doing on this train?'

'I've been up in Town having a chin-chin with my governor.

By the way! did you say anything to him about my having a 'plane of my own when he was down at the club last week?'

'He asked me what I thought about it,' Robert answered, 'and I told him.'

'What?'

'I said I thought you'd break your neck in it, having wasted a lot of money first.'

'Harsh words, RO, harsh words.'

'True words, Mastley, true words.'

He sighed.

'I suppose you're right. Anyhow, the Old Boy's refused to stump up.'

'And so your dreams of shooting up the neighbourhood will never be anything more?'

'I've seen you flying pretty low at times!'

'I've done enough flying.'

'I suppose it does make a difference.'

'You bet it does.'

Mastley yawned and stretched himself.

'What time does this train get into the junction?'

''Fraid I don't know.'

'Ten fifty-four,' said the clerk.

'Oh – er – thanks.'

'You – fly?' continued the clerk.

'Yes,' Robert answered when his companion made no reply.

'It must be wonderful to fly!' ventured the girl.

'It is,' Robert said.

'Wasn't it very cold work at this time of year?' asked the clerk.

'Sometimes,' Mastley said.

'Have you ever done a parachute jump?' inquired the girl.

'No,' said Mastley, 'but he has,' and he jerked his head towards Robert.

'I say, have you really?'

'Yes. I did a drop once.'

'What was it like?' the clerk leaned forward in his seat.

'I was frightened, but there was nothing in it.'

'So he says,' murmured Mastley.

'Do you go up every day?' the girl went on. Mastley nodded.

'It's just a job,' Robert said, 'only it happens to be the finest job in the world.'

'I've always wanted to fly,' said the clerk.

'You'd be ill,' the girl grimaced.

'He'd only be sick the first couple of times,' Robert said.

The clerk began to undo his rucksack. 'I've tons of bread-and-cheese here,' he said. 'I wonder if – if you'd care to join us?'

'I'm not very hungry, I had –' Mastley began.

'Thank you," said Robert, 'we'll surely join you. I've some bottled beer in my bag when it comes to washing it down.'

The girl nibbled at a hunk of cheese. 'Are you in the Air Force?' she asked.

'Not now, I used to be,' Robert answered.

'He's a flying instructor,' said Mastley. 'You ought to hear him swearing through the telephones when he's teaching me aerobatics.'

'That's stunting, isn't it?'

'Yes.'

'Do you teach it?'

'I do,' Robert answered, laughing.

'You must have nerves like steel.'

He laughed again. 'There's nothing in them at all so long as they're done above a couple of thousand feet. Flying's not dangerous, you know!'

'Look at all those that get killed!' said the girl.

'That's newspaper publicity.'

'I've always wanted to learn to fly,' said the clerk.

'You may get the chance yet,' said Robert. 'At the moment

it's too darned expensive, but I hope to see the day when any bloke who wants to can get into the air when he wants to and where he wants to.'

'There won't be much kick left in flying then,' put in Mastley.

'What about women?' the girl asked.

'They don't make good pilots as a rule, though I've had one very good woman pupil.'

The clerk opened the bottle of beer Robert gave him with a penny and handed it to his companion. 'There's a great future for aviation, isn't there?' he asked.

'I don't know,' Mastley said. 'What do you think about it, RO?'

'It's very hard to tell,'? Robert said, 'because the aeroplane has suffered from forced growth owing to its use as an offensive military weapon. As a result of this, hardly any form of commercial aviation is a paying proposition when Government subsidy is taken away. Then you have the attitude of the man-in-the-street who thinks of the aeroplane as a form of flying motor-car and expects its development to be analogous. I hope that flying will develop, but as things are now I don't see much prospect of it doing so.'

'That's rather a glum view, isn't it?' said the clerk.

'Flying's no use, anyhow,' Robert answered.

'Oh, I say, that's laying it on a bit thick!' Mastley broke in.

'I've never heard that said before,' said the girl.

'Well, is it?'? Robert continued. 'Has flying made the world a better place to live in?'

'Not yet,' said the clerk, 'not yet, certainly.'

'If it's all this,' said the girl quickly, 'why are you so fond of it?'

'First, because it is useless. Life itself is useless, a struggle without purpose. Flying to-day is no more than a form of warfare. I, for example, was trained in the Royal Air Force, and the club which now employs me would fail without

Government aid. Now war is a part of life, a befitting end to an inane struggle, to those endless variations on a theme which form our existence. I say this because he who dies in war dies fighting what is probably the only thing there is no need for him to fight; his fellow man. So the absurdity of human existence is drawn out to its illogical conclusion.

'Second, because flying is what I call an intensification of life. Every facet of living: courage, danger, despair, exhilaration, comradeship, the perception of beauty, contemplation, individualism, the joy of speed, the influence of weather, is heightened many times when one flies.'

'It's wonderful what a beer does to you,' said Mastley, after a pause.

The girl looked at her companion. 'Do you really think there's going to be a war?'

'I hope not,' said Robert, as he opened another bottle of beer. 'I hope not.'

The Fifteenth Chapter

1

The finest summer for many years had burnt the grass before the apron so that a great wave of dust swirled into the hangars as Judy ran up the engine of the new Gipsy Moth. Robert pushed home the locking pin of his Sutton harness. 'Wave the chocks away and taxi her out. We'll see how much you can remember.'

The Moth bumped gently across the aerodrome, swerving to bursts of throttle and violent ruddering. 'You should have come down before,' he went on. 'It's been hell only seeing you once a week through all these months.' He looked up into the mirror as he spoke and saw her smile. She turned the aircraft into wind. He scanned the sky once more, reminded her to set the cheese-cutter and held the controls lightly, waiting for her to take off.

In all the long hours of a day's work each action of a pupil had to be carefully watched, every manoeuvre anticipated, all movements of the controls checked. Through all the dreary repetition of circuits, spins, blind-flying and aerobatics an instructor could never for one second allow his mental picture of the pupil's purpose to grow dim in outline, blurred in detail.

They climbed up into the clear sky above the simmering haze of a June afternoon. He began to correct her turns, telling her that she was holding off too much bank. Then he made her spin left and right and finally return to the aerodrome for landings.

'How am I doing?'

'Not too badly.'

'Don't lie to me. I always know when you're pleased!'

'Do you, indeed?'

'M'm – you whistle softly – usually the slow march from Handel's *Scipio*.'

She tried a landing in the corner by the petrol pumps. 'You're holding off too high,' he said, 'and you're still a darn sight too stiff on those ruddy controls. Now take her round again and try another. Remember what I told you about holding off too much bank on a turn.'

As she throttled down to eighteen hundred over the golf course Judy remarked that an instructor's anticipation of a pupil's mistakes was one of the things about learning to fly that particularly impressed her. He pulled the mouthpiece up to his chin. 'There's nothing in it. The majority of pupils fall into one or two categories and each crowd makes the same sort of mistakes.'

This understanding of another, he thought, was but the realization of blunders common to types of embryonic aviators. In that it was as other forms of physical, mental and spiritual intimacy, aggravating in its fleeting, incomplete perfection.

Again Judy throttled back, held the 'plane in a steady glide, turned in to land, eased the stick back ... back ... back ... as the ground rose up to meet her, dropping the aircraft for a perfect landing.

'Not bad, not bad at all. Three more like that and you can do some solo.'

2

Judy came down to the aerodrome on every fine day during the seven weeks which followed. In the afternoons she would go up alone; flying with Robert in the evenings when the earth was blotched with elongated shadows and a turn brought swift bars of darkness across their faces, so low was the sun behind the interplane struts. He taught her side-slipping and instrument flying. He taught her to fly by compass, showing her speed error and northerly turning error, bawling incessantly till she could fly a good course, nagging till she map-read intelligently and could be trusted on long solo cross-country flights.

When their dual was over they would taxi straight into the hangars, grinning at Perkins, who would be locking up the petrol pumps. Then they would go into the lighted clubhouse for supper, into the glare and laughter that ever seemed a strange contrast to the spacious emptiness of the heavens. And after chatting at the bar and dancing with social members he would run Judy into Best to catch the late London train.

On Wednesday it was Robert's turn to instruct in night flying. As very few of the 'A' pilots were to be trusted up alone in the darkness, this meant that he did innumerable circuits, always turning from the path of flares that marked the aerodrome and the scar of light that was the clubhouse to follow with weary eyes the tiny glowworm of the train that carried Judy back to London.

He would think of it, windows gleaming in a regular line, steam ruddy with the glow of the engine fire, ripping into the night. And then he would imagine her, see her seated in her corner, one foot twisted about another, hands clasping some book he had given her, her slim, firm body swaying with the rocking of the train. She would be gazing thoughtfully into the night, her head tilted backwards on the slender pillar of her neck, blue eyes half closed, her hair smooth as weir water in the strong, metallic light.

As he thought of these things his pupil would make some mistake, show signs of hesitation or apprehension and he would lean forward, cursing through the telephones, his mind once more cloaked by responsibility.

3

Robert swung himself into his Morris and slammed the door. 'There's been a level-crossing collision somewhere down the line. The London train will be about two hours late.'

Judy nodded.

'I think coffee would be a stout idea.' He touched the self-starter knob. Instantly the engine rippled into life, its lazy note drowning the crash of milk cans, the melancholic chatter of taxi drivers, the far-away muttering of a train. He drove through the dead streets of the city and parked the car outside the principal restaurant. The main room was half full, for the audience had just left the theatre that stood across the road. Judy led him to a table by the window. A panorama of the town lay before them, dominated by the grim, static mass of the Cathedral. Robert ordered coffee and biscuits.

'What's that thing they're playing on the radio gramophone?'

'I don't know,' Robert said.

'Don't be lazy – what is it?'

'Chausson's *Poéme*.'

'You're a queer fellow, Robert.'

'Thank you, my dear.'

'One moment you're quoting a line such as Wilfred Owen's "Courage was mine, and I had mystery" and the next you're roaring over some dirty story with Martin. You like Beethoven, don't you?'

'I like Beethoven.'

'And you like playing skittles for pints?'

'And I like playing skittles for pints. I'm an ordinary man. There are very few of us left.'

In the street below a boy and girl were kissing in the seclusion of a shop doorway. A beggar passed down the gutter searching for cigarette ends. A cyclist went by, head down, pushing an oblong of light before him on the roadway.

A man at a neighbouring table was patting the wall with the palm of his hand. One panel was hot but the next was quite cool, he said. A waitress answered that this was due to the use of asbestos behind a fireplace on the other side of the wall.

'Robert?'

'M'm.'

'You've loved other women, haven't you?'

'No.'

'Well, you've told them you loved them?'

'Sometimes.'

'And when you told them that, did you think you loved them?'

'Sometimes.'

'Is it going to be that way with me?'

'What way?'

'Don't be stupid. If someone says to you when you're old, "Have you ever been in love?" are you going to say, "No, but I thought I was"?'

'No, Judy. I love you. God knows why, but I do.'

'And I love you, Robert.'

'It's surely fine to be in love. Sometimes when I can't sleep and it's cold and black and I feel afraid to die, I think to myself, "Soon she'll be by my side, I shall put out my hand and touch her and there'll be an end of loneliness". Then I feel happy and slide down into sleep once more.'

She leaned forward for him to light her cigarette. He saw her forehead crinkle into a frown, heard her sigh very softly. She smiled when he asked what was the matter and shook her head.

'Nothing, my dear.'

So it is, he thought, that even in love we live apart, shut into our own lives. As the years go by we will grow familiar with each other's tricks of speech and habits of mind, till broken phrases suffice for conversation, till an expression tells of a mood. Even then our understanding will be at the best physical, emotional, a thing imperfect, condemning us to spiritual loneliness. We shall be as two pilots flying wing tip to wing tip who, for all their nearness and understanding each of the other, can only communicate by clumsy and laborious effort.

4

'More compass exercises?' Judy asked as she walked towards the Tiger Moth.

'No,' Robert said. 'You're flying fairly well by compass now, so we'll make a start on aerobatics.'

'Aerobatics?'

'M'm.'

'What use are they?'

'No use at all.'

'Then why do I have to do 'em?'

'To teach you flying for the sake of flying, pure aviation and all that.' He put two cushions in the back seat and helped her into the rear cockpit.

'My dear! you look dreadfully tired,' she said, as he pulled on her Sutton harness.

'Done over six hours' dual already. The last bloke I took up couldn't hear, though I'd taken special care to see that his ear-phones fitted. Nothing wears one out so much as bawling through the tubes and getting no response.'

As she took off he told her to climb to three thousand feet and leaned his head against the rest, happy to be away from the foreshortened familiarity of the aerodrome, to have finished with circuits for another day.

They flew eastwards so that the mellow sunshine made each of the instruments into a mirror and he could see a reflection of his face, framed by a dirty linen helmet, topped by heavy goggles, in the glass of the ASI. He looked up into the real mirror which was set on a centre section strut so as to give him a view of his pupil's face. Judy was sitting as far forward as her straps would allow, concentrating on holding the 'plane in a steady climb. Unlike Robert she wore her goggles in position. She looked like a youth, he thought, happily enthusiastic in her rough clothing.

At three thousand feet she levelled off.

'I've got her,' Robert said. 'Have you done any aerobatics before? No, of course not. Routine question. Sorry. Well, there's nothing to worry about. I'll begin with a loop.' He watched her as he dived, eased the aircraft up and over the top, throttled back and fell out. Her hands clutched the cockpit doors, her lips were parted, showing even, clenched teeth.

'There was nothing in that, was there?'

'Only a funny feeling going up – I had no sensation of being upside down.'

'Of course not. The centripetal force holds you in your seat. Now do one with me. First we dive to get the necessary speed. Be careful not to over-rev the engine. At about a hundred and twelve – throttle full open and up we go.' The horizon dropped from sight, the engine note grew more shrill. 'The nose drifts a bit to the left, so we want some right rudder. Now the other horizon comes round. Throttle closed, ease the stick gently forward coming out. There's nothing in it. Do you follow me?'

'What was that you said about rudder?'

'You have to work out what rudder you want as you go over. Be careful how you put the stick forward coming out or you'll pull the wings off. Do you follow me?'

'I follow you.'

'Right. Do one yourself. Now a good look round the sky first, then over you go!'

She dived, pushed the throttle wide open, eased the nose up till the Moth was standing on its tail.

'Get the stick back!'

She made no movement.

'Get the stick BACK!'

There was still no movement of the controls.

'GET THE STICK BACK!' He grinned at her frightened reflection in the mirror. 'All right, I've got her.' He stall turned out.

'What was the matter that time?'

'Wind up. I've never seen so much sky in my life.'

He laughed. 'Well, try another, will you? Remember that I'm always at hand to help you.'

She looped, and he said, 'Not bad at all, except that you slammed the throttle back as you came over the top. Climb, up and do some more.'

Quarter of an hour later they returned to the aerodrome, Judy flushed with pride at having done five perfect loops.

'Let me have her, will you?' He flew over the centre of the landing field. 'Have you got your straps on tight?'

'M'm.'

'Right. I'm going to chuck her about a bit.' He dived, pulled up the nose and slow half-rolled, centralizing the controls when the 'plane was flying inverted.

'Robert! I'm hanging off the seat!'

'Of course you are. Follow my movements on the controls and don't try to hold yourself in.' He dived out. Spun. Flick half-rolled. Stall turned. Half-rolled off a loop. 'How d'you feel?'

'Frightened.'

'Not sick?'

'No.'

'Good. I'll make an aerobatic pilot of you yet.'

'You won't. I'm too frightened, especially in flick half-rolling, when the whole 'plane corkscrews over.'

'Nonsense. You'll get used to it.'

'Not to the feeling of the kite running away with me.'

'Tripe! Now you've got her. Do a nice landing.'

She landed the Moth on the circle, smiling as the hollow rumbling sound of the tail-skid told her that the landing had been a good one.

'How was that?'

'You certainly knew where the ground was.' He too smiled as he spoke, thinking of the aerobatics he would teach her. Through her gradual mastery of his branch of flying, through her increasing disregard of fear and attendant growth of confidence, of skill, of judgement, he would be supremely happy. But when she had obtained a nominal proficiency, when the object of his desire was within his grasp, he knew that he would lose all but professional interest, hating his petty triumph for its easy winning.

5

The test pilot who was selected out of many applicants to fill Metcalf's place was a big Yorkshireman named Bettington. His sandy hair was thin. He had been flying for fifteen years, and his career included six years in the Air Force, air-taxi work in the Near East and test piloting at home. He always spoke of having 'fled' a 'plane and had a habit of flying between the hangars that upset the club Committee. Lack of exercise had made him fat; drink and weather had coarsened his features. But he was still a good pilot and able to pass his medical boards without difficulty. He had intensely blue eyes, a laugh like the stroke of a saw and big hands with square-tipped fingers.

As the summer went by he became very fond of the clubhouse, and would spend his evenings at the bar, and bad weather days in the instructors' room. He grew very familiar with Martin and they would stand for hours at the bar counter exchanging samples of pantagruelism in undertones, occasionally breaking into loud laughter.

Judy disliked him from the start.

'There's something I don't like about that man,' she said to Robert one evening as they came into the club-house for supper.

'He's a good pilot.'

'That covers everything, doesn't it?'

'Almost. He's been rather a bad lad where women are concerned, I'm told.'

'Not like you, sweet?'

'Not like me.'

'How fortunate I was to meet you!'

'Not that I haven't been tempted.'

'You tempted?'

'It was on a ship coming home through the Mediterranean. It was Christmas and the moon was shining on the water and I was young!'

'Poor boy!'

'She had red hair. She was ravishing. She stood in the entrance to her cabin. She said, 'Come in and have a drink, George!'

'Real champagne?'

'I remembered the old school. I remembered the Bishop's words at my confirmation. Judy! I passed that woman by.'

'And now?'

'My strength is as the strength of ten. What will you have to drink while we wait for ham-and-eggs?'

'A gin-and-lime, please.'

When he pushed his way through the crowd with her drink she was sitting in the window at their favourite table.

'Happy, my dear?'

She smiled at him over the rim of her glass.

'It was in this clubhouse we first met,' he went on.

'I haven't forgotten it.'

'You wore tweeds and had a hand-bag with a model airscrew sewn on to it –'

'And you were very curt –'

'At having a rich woman pupil.'

She took a cigarette from his case and tapped it absently on the table. Bettington's voice ripped through a general pause in the chatter. 'Good Lord, no! I was so embarrassed after that first time that I didn't go near a woman for six months' – he stopped as Martin nudged him, a roar of laughter submerging his confusion. Judy touched Robert's hand and looked towards the open French windows. He followed her glance. Mastley stood in the opening, the sight of his approach having been masked by the dusk, the sound by the general uproar. He was green in the face and leaned against the frame, arms hanging limply from the shoulders. His linen helmet lay loosely on his neck. He made no sound. Robert led him to his table and got him a drink.

'What's the matter?'

'I've just been in an inverted spin and only got out by accident.'

'The hell you have,' Robert said.

'My straps weren't very tight either. It shook me up, I can tell you. Then coming in to land I dropped the kite from twenty feet into the far corner of the aerodrome.'

'Did you bend it?'

'Yes. A longeron's gone and a wing's collapsed.'

'Who's out there?'

'No-one.'

'No-one?'

'No. You're the first person I've told.'

'Where's Perkins?'

'Don't know.'

'Look after him, Judy.' He went into the instructors' room and emerged with Heylead. Together they rounded up the mechanics and sent them out to handle the 'plane in. The light had gone, and when he followed them out he could hear the chain of their voices stretching out into the darkness, see patches of light floating down one side of the aerodrome. The boy was still sitting with Judy when he returned. His beer was untouched.

'Drink it up,' Robert said, 'and tell me all about it. But first, who gave you permission to take a kite up so late?'

'Perkins did.'

'Perkins? He'd no right.'

'I know, but you were flying, and I didn't want to ask Heylead.'

You didn't want to ask Heylead, Robert thought, because you damn well knew he wouldn't let you go up.

'I see. Now about the inverted spin?'

'Well, I'd never done one, but I thought I'd have a crack at it. Bettington told me what to do –'

'Did he, indeed?'

'Yes. I dived the kite to a hundred and five, pulled the nose well up, put on full bank with a touch of bottom rudder and throttled back as I went on to my back.'

'That's all right.'

'He'd told me how important it was to get the stick forward when I was upside down. I shoved it forward all right, but took the bank off. I stuck there for an age. Then I began to come off very slowly. I suppose I hadn't taken all the bank off. I remembered about rudder, "plenty of rudder", Bettington said. Then she kicked like hell and spun with the nose up and me hanging head down by the straps. It was hell, RO.'

'What height?'

'I started at about eighteen hundred feet.'

'Someone looks after you blokes,' Robert said.

'Then I kicked the rudder central and pulled the stick into my stomach. I remembered hearing someone say that that was the way to get out. I was in the deuce of a funk and was shouting at myself, "Rudder central – stick back. Rudder central – stick back". Then she came out screaming. I was just above the trees. When I came in to land it was getting dark and I was all shaken up and – well – I bent it.'

'I've got them to put flares out,' Robert said. 'I'm going to take you up again in a few minutes. You'd better get a coat, it'll be cold now the sun's gone down.'

'Gosh!' he said to Judy when the boy had gone into the locker room, 'has that lad put me in a spot?'

The Sixteenth Chapter

1

It seemed to Robert that there had never been such weather in England. Every day was clear when the morning haze lifted, every day was still, cloudless, sun-filled, so that they flew from ten till dusk. Every day the aerodrome was busy with club activities, with joy-riding, the arrival and departure of air liners, test flying and squadron exercises.

One morning he awoke to the sound of rain drifting against his window. By eleven it was clear again and he went up on test. But the clouds were all about him and an approaching storm forced him to hedge-hop back to the aerodrome. As he landed, mechanics running out to catch his wing tips, he saw Bearing climbing out of a Puss Moth which had been taxied into the main hangar. He reported to Heylead and joined his old pupil at the bar.

'Hullo!'

'Hullo, RO! What are you having?'

'Coffee, please?'

'Not a man's drink?'

'Never touch it in the daytime.'

'Of course, I'd forgotten. How's things?'

'So-so. And you?'

'Much the same. I'm mugging up for second-class navigator's.'

'All the best.'

'Thanks. Not that I'm worried. I've only failed twice. Most of the lads are in double figures.'

'I thought you were flying on the Irish ferry?'

'I was, but they went bang a week ago.'

'I hadn't heard.'

'Yes. I'm doing odd jobs now. Joy-riding and taxi work when the trips are short enough. Flew a retired colonel down this morning.'

'That red-faced bird I saw in the hangars?'

'That's the bloke. Queer old stick. Insisted on talking Imperialism all the way down while I was trying to fly by DR. I felt like bawling at him to shut up. I don't mind dying for England, but I bloody well object to slobbering over her.'

The barman brought the coffee.

'Pleased to see you again, sir.'

'Thank you, Symmons.'

'Turning out wet, sir.'

'It is. How are things in the booze racket?'

'Not too bad, sir.'

Robert picked up a charity novelty from the counter and began to push in squares through the tray. Five attempts brought no response and he dropped sixpence into a tumbler set aside for the purpose.

'Has anyone won anything from that thing since I left?'

'No,' Robert said.

'I suppose nothing else has changed either?'

'We've got a new chief instructor.'

'Oh yes. I've heard about him. Bit of a nancy-boy, isn't he?'

'He has his moments.'

'How d'you get on?'

'We don't. Had a grand row about a month ago after a pupil of mine, a bloke called Mastley, piled up a kite. He'd taken it up without permission. I was flying at the time. Heylead tried to pin the blame on to me.'

'Tough,' commented the other, 'tough. By the way, I ran into Judy Hateling at a first night last week. She told me she's coming down here again.'

'Rather. She's getting good too. You ought to see her slow rolls!'

'Smooth as a baby's bottom?'

'You've taken the very words out of my mouth.'

Bearing tapped his cup on the edge of his saucer.

'Her husband's gone West, hasn't he?'

Robert looked at him sharply. 'What have you heard?'

'Only that you both – go about a bit.'

'Our engagement will be announced one of these days.'

'I'm glad. Congrats, old man.'

'Thanks.' He went to the windows to look at the weather. 'As a matter of fact, she's indirectly the cause of another row between Heylead and myself.'

'How come?'

'Oh, he said something about our being seen too much together. I was very tired and made a crack about his seventeen and sixpenny friends.'

'He's that sort, is he?'

'He is.'

'So things, I take it, are slightly strained?'

'Strained is the word.'

'There won't be any flying for an hour or two,' said Bearing. 'What about having the gloves on?'

'OK with me.'

A few minutes later they were squaring up in the hangar. They grinned at one another. Robert led, his opponent countered, feinted, brought his left across. Robert ducked and swung in a right hook, knocking Bearing's head back. They clinched and were broken by Perkins. Robert smiled as he fought, happy in the control of temper, the joy of inflicting pain, his mind sharpened by fear. In his mouth was the sweet taste of blood, he could hear only the thud of glove on flesh and the cries of the mechanics who had gathered round. Suddenly Perkins whistled through his teeth.

'Look out – here's the chief.'

There was a scurrying of the mechanics back to their benches. The two stopped boxing, Bearing leaning on Robert's arm. They were both breathing deeply, a continuous sound which formed a background to the hollow footsteps of the chief instructors. Perkins stood quite still, feet apart, watch in hand, chin on chest, looking at his superior from under his eyebrows.

'Mr Owen!' Heylead's voice was confidently petulant; it was the voice of a schoolmaster being authoritative with a boy who dare not answer back. 'Mr Owen! do you realize that even if there is no flying, you're still on duty?'

So it is, thought Robert, in all the great moments of our lives; in anger, in passion, in achievement, so it is in fear, in hope, in lust, in sorrow and in death. In all these climaxes we become ridiculous in our pricked importance, theatrical in our intense egoism. And these happenings, which give lilt to our existence, influence the whole of our days, forming the outline of the farce we call life.

'Mr Owen! Do you realize that you're on duty?'

'So are you, you sod!' He hit the chief instructor on the mark as he spoke and knocked him out with a right to the jaw. He fell awkwardly, blood running from one corner of his mouth.

'Neat,' said Perkins. 'Neat.'

Bearing began to untie his gloves with his teeth. 'It's a nice time of the year to be looking for work,' he said.

2

After midday the weather cleared, flying re-commenced and the clubhouse began to fill with the usual crowd of social members. Robert watched them as he waited for a pupil. There were fat old men, gossiping over their drinks. There were pretty girls sipping gin with the correct ennui. There were middle-aged women screaming with make-up, their flabby bodies crammed into figure foundations, their feet rammed into shoes a size too small. There were young men, flying members, who would have been thrown out of a Royal Air Force Flying Training School in a week. To keep these people in this useful state, he thought, thousands of men worked in mines, at milling machines, at office desks, in shops, in ships at sea; thousands of girls worked at office desks, behind counters, at bars, in factories, in cotton mills. This picture of the sweating masses supporting the idle rich pleased him. He knew it was out of perspective, as Van Gogh's *Vincent's Chair*, but he felt in the mood to be pleased by building up an argument on a fundamental defect.

About three o'clock he saw Judy standing on the apron as he landed. She waited until he had gone over the lesson with his pupil and then joined her.

'Can you take me up now?'

''Fraid not, my dear. There's been something wrong with 'RN's' compass. Perkins has been playing with it and now I've got to take it up and fly on known bearings.'

'Can I have the Tiger Moth to do some solo aerobatics?'

'Help yourself. Don't go a long way from the aerodrome, and if the weather comes on thick, as it looks like doing, run for home!'

As he went into the clubhouse for knee-pad and pencil he saw Martin coming in through the rear door of the bar.

'Hullo – what're you doing down here?'

'I've got an extra half – the exams are on. Where's the chief instructor? I want to see about my renewal of licence.'

'He's got a headache,' Robert said, 'he'll be back in a day or so.'

'I always suspected the man was effeminate, now I know it.'

'Flying this afternoon?'

'I should say so. Can you give me a spot of dual on forced landings?'

'I'm sorry, but I'm booked up. We didn't fly this morning, so there's a lot to do.'

'Can Bettington take me up?'

'You'll have to ask Major Yeates about that, he's in the Control Office. If he gives you leave, for heaven's sake go easy on the split-arse stuff.'

'That, coming from you, is good.'

'It's meant, nevertheless.'

He got into the Gipsy Moth, waved away the chocks and took off cross wind, wrenching the aircraft into a steep turn as he left the ground so that the wing tip seemed to sweep the grass. A few seconds later he, turned again, flying over the clubhouse with his wheels skimming the gaudy tiles. He looked down at the startled faces with a distaste that was new. In a fortnight he would have finished there. Although the Major had murmured a conventional protest when receiving the notice, Robert thought he had seen an expression of relief in the old man's eyes. The chief instructor had already lodged a protest and a committee meeting had been called in consequence.

At two thousand feet he flew level. He turned the 'plane on to a known bearing, unclamped the compass, twisted the grid ring, checked the bearing on the lubber line. In fourteen days, he thought, he would be out of a job. Well, he had been out of a job before.

Half a mile away Judy was doing aerobatics. She began with a stall turn, went on to loop, half-rolled and then began a slow roll. He watched her, glancing from time to time at his compass. The Tiger Moth climbed steeply, fell again as it rolled on to its back, came out lazily with the loss of two hundred feet or so. He smiled, for she was flying well and his handiwork pleased him.

Then she began another slow roll, but centralized the controls when upside down and continued gliding inverted. Robert began to test his compass for speed error. When he looked up again she was still flying upside down. He thought he could see the blob of her head hanging down from the fuselage. Suddenly he noticed another Gipsy Moth at a higher altitude. As he followed it the nose went down and it began to glide. It was Bettington and Martin doing a forced landing. They were going to go damn close to Judy. Steady! he thought, one can't judge from here. But what if they're both watching the field? If they come down on top of her, it's the end. Even if she had a parachute she'd be stunned by the impact. I tell you it's all right, you bloody fool, they'll pass with a hundred yards of daylight between them. You can't judge from here. Bettington knows his job, he'd be bound to look below before throttling back.

Then he knew that they were going to collide. He put on bank to the right as his port wing obscured the two aircraft. 'Judy!' he screamed, 'Judy! for sweet Christ's sake!' His voice was lost in the engine's roar, his words swept away in the slipstream.

The impact, being noiseless to him, was quite unreal. He saw part of the Tiger Moth break away and flutter downwards, he saw the 'plane itself spinning earthwards, he saw the Gipsy Moth continuing to fly level. He throttled back and dived his aircraft till the wind shrieked in the wires. Judy's Moth was much below him now and it seemed that it must spin into the ground at every second. Then he saw it fold into the corner of a long narrow field. He noticed that the field ran across the wind and was surrounded by big trees, each standing in the pool of its own shadow. He sideslipped violently, landed inside the hedge and taxied as near the debris as he dared. As he climbed out of the cockpit he heard an aero engine, and, looking upwards, saw the other Moth limping back to the aerodrome, its undercarriage hanging in useless wreckage.

The Tiger Moth had not caught fire. It was telescoped, and he had considerable difficulty in releasing Judy. Her clothes were blood-soaked and she moaned when he touched her. He put her to lie on the ground, propping her head on a mole hill that he covered with the blind-flying hood. She wasn't going to die, one couldn't die on such a lovely day.

He went on to the road at the other end of the field and stopped a car.

'I see that you belong to the AA. Have you got your key?'

'Yes.' The driver was a youth, gazing at Robert with some alarm.

'There's been a bad aeroplane crash in that field and a lady is badly injured. Will you 'phone from the box at the next cross-roads?'

'Of course.'

'Ring up Dr. Towsler, Best 168. Tell him to get out to a field just south of the Langley cross-roads. Tell him it's life or death. Then 'phone the aerodrome, Best 297, tell them to send the ambulance out to a field just south of the Langley cross-roads and that a kite – an aeroplane – is coming in to land with a damaged undercart. Get it?'

The youth repeated the messages and drove off. Robert ran back to the wrecked 'plane.

Judy began to recover consciousness.

'It's awful – this pain. How – long are they going to be?'

'Not long.'

For the next half-hour she asked the question again and again, and he would walk to the fence and returning, lie to her, saying that he could see them beyond the cross-roads.

She moaned and writhed, asking him to take her coat off, to do something to stop the pain. Motorists gathered round. One gave Robert some brandy. He diluted a very small quantity and gave it to Judy, her teeth rattling against the neck of the flask.

The doctor arrived, and after him the ambulance driven by Perkins. The doctor gave her morphia hypodermically and was very busy for some minutes. Then he got her on to a stretcher and loaded it into the ambulance. When a mechanic had driven it away Robert asked Perkins about the other Gipsy Moth.

'They crashed, but they weren't hurt,' the GE said. 'What about your kite?' he went on.

'What about it?'? Robert said.

'Well, you can't fly it out of here!'

'Oh, can't I?'

'But, Mr Owen –'

'I want you to look after the debris. I'll arrange for a lorry to be sent out.'

'Yes, Mr Owen.'

Perkins swung the airscrew and Robert took off down the field. He saw the trees drifting towards his port wing tips and swore, putting the 'plane into a vertical which brushed his wheels against the leaves.

The Seventeenth Chapter

1

The waiting-room was at the rear of the nursing home, a severe, narrow room with tall windows, frosted to hide the backyard, wooden chairs that moved with squealed protest on the polished linoleum and a large dining-room table covered with out-of-date magazines. The alcove that had held a kitchen range was covered by painted plywood at the base of which stood a minute gas fire. One windowsill held a row of books that had been left behind by patients. Robert noticed several best sellers, a few biographies, a cookery book, a Bible, a railway guide and a child's rag book. He was still wearing his dirty linen flying-suit and sat without movement, his eyes forever on the door. On the other side of the table was a small mouse-like woman who turned the pages of a Society journal unceasingly. There was no need for them to speak, he thought. Sorrow had given them a bitter comradeship that transcended every barrier of modern life.

The matron came in.

'Mr Owen!'

He got to his feet, put helmet and goggles on the table and followed her down the passage. There was a good deal of bustle about the home. A shrill bell rang almost incessantly, nurses moved from room to room, from floor to floor. Everywhere there was a smell of antiseptic and floor polish. When they reached the second floor she led him down the landing. They passed an open door. A golden-haired child who played with coloured wooden bricks glanced up at him for a second, interest freezing all movement, and then went on heaping up a pyramid on his counterpane. As they reached the end of the landing the grey-haired woman told him to wait.

'How is she, matron?'

'She's very bad.'

She went in and shut the door. His hands were damp with sweat. He understood why men pray. The door opened. Someone told him that he could go in. It was a big room, empty of furniture except for a tiny dressing table and the bed which was hidden by a screen. Doctor Towsler was standing in a corner talking to a nurse. He beckoned to Robert.

'She's very bad – only a minute –' Robert nodded. The matron had gone behind the screen and was talking in a low voice. He failed to distinguish her words, but her tone was mechanically reassuring, easily cheerful. He went round the screen. When he saw Judy fear rolled in a great wave inside him. She was crying: 'Robert! Robert! Oh, Robert! put your arms around me!' Her voice was a tired whisper.

He stood still, afraid to touch her broken body that was swollen with dressings, bandages, splints. She cried with a passive helplessness, the tears running down to the bandage at her throat. He leaned over, smoothed her hair and kissed her. Her breath was sweet with chloroform.

'Robert?'

'Yes.'

' ... nearer ...'

'What is it?'

'I'm ... afraid.'

'There's nothing to be afraid of.'

'Don't leave me ... I'm ... afraid.'

'I won't leave you,' he said. The moments dragged by. 'Are you – in pain?'

'Not ... now ... it was ... cruel ... cruel ...'

The noises of the home were faint and far-away. In the next house a wireless blared out a popular comedian's inanity. Occasionally there was the 'clonk-clack' of a loose manhole cover in the road being disturbed by a tyre. Judy began to hum loudly. The matron came over and touched his sleeve. He let go her bandaged hand and went away.

Fifteen minutes later he saw her again. Her face was grey. She was unconscious. He went back to the waiting-room, and in a little while the doctor came down and said that she was dead.

2

'... *Man that is born of woman hath but a short time to live, and is full of misery. He cometh up, and is cut down, like a flower; he fleeth as it were a shadow ...*'

The wind, laden with rain, blew away the priest's words, sent loose leaves from Robert's prayer book fluttering on to the sodden, red earth that stained the chief mourners' boots.

It is not the fact of death itself, he thought, that overwhelms us and glooms the future. The sudden and final parting has its counterpart in life; much of our sorrow is self-pity. As to the future, even if we never forget, memory distorts the actuality, making it at the best a colourful dream, at the worst a horror dimmed by the passing of the years. It is the unfinished hopes, the awakening from dreams that can never be realized. It is the emptiness of future living, the resolution never to turn in one's tracks and gaze sentimentally backwards.

'... *We give thee hearty thanks for that it hath pleased thee to deliver this our sister out of the miseries of this sinful world ...*'

3

The sun was setting as the train left the first of the four tunnels and the estuary wheeled into Robert's sight. As every moment brought a change in the light on the water, so he knew that every hour of the fickle weather played tricks with the purple fastness of the hills that were heaped up on the other side of the river.

He might have been a boy returning from school so eagerly did he watch for the first glimpse of the towered island, the line of fishing boats, the ferry refuge set in the golden haze of the dunes on the opposite shore.

He left his luggage in the dusk-filled station and walked past the rocks where the swirling, green tide tugged at the strong-smelling seaweed; past the terrace whose gardens, burnt with summer, ran down to the water. He went past the harbour where big, grey seagulls perched on the broken wooden breakwater that was green with seaweed and crucified against the sunset.

A lamplighter went before him down the road climbing each post in turn, chaining the soft darkness with the hissing, yellow lights. As he went by the mussel tanks, the life-boat house, the hanging nets, he heard the ragged lilt of Welsh, the faint crying of a gull, the stir of the tide running over the bar, the staccato commands of the ferryman rolling over the placid water as his assistant moored the motor-boat for the night.

A steamer was tied up at the landing-stage, its lights meretricious against the pale stars. The shops threw out hoods of light that caught the strolling visitors for fleeting seconds, accentuating their bright clothing.

Late that evening his father emptied the ivory chessmen on to the board; set them in their places with leisurely dexterity. 'Red or white?'

'Red.'

'I like the red the better, too,' his father said, 'they seem to bring me luck.'

They began to play, the little carved figures becoming for each of them the centre of his world. When the game was ended his father became intent on resetting the pieces.

'You've got a holiday, Robert?'

'No. I lost the job I had at Best.'

'Have you got another?'

'Yes, Father.'

'A flying job?' his father asked, turning the board very carefully so as not to upset the men.

'Yes, a flying job.'

'When d'you go?'

'In a few days.'

His father sighed.

'This time you have the first move.'

The Last Chapter

He led his pupil to the second 'plane in the third row of Tiger Moths. Taking his parachute from the lower wing he pulled on the quick-release harness, motioning the boy to get into the rear cockpit. Everywhere engines were being started and run up, the slipstream of many airscrews blowing grass and bits of paper against the white concrete buildings of the Reserve school. A refuelling unit, coupled to a Hucks' starter, moved down the lane between the Moths. Across the aerodrome a squadron of Auxiliary Air Force Bombers waited, tall aircraft, a cold silver in the sunshine, alive with mechanics.

Over to the right were the test beds where mighty nine-hundred horse-power engines roared their unused paean as caged beasts that forever move about their tiny spaces.

He watched his pupil, a Sergeant Pilot of the Royal Air Force Reserve, as the latter tried to remember all the things he had been taught during his ground course.

'You'll have to get your straps on tighter than that. Pull the seat up against them.'

The boy nodded. He had keen, intelligent features, the arrogant confidence of youth tempered by slight fear.

'Have you ever flown before?'

'Never, sir.'

'Right. I want you to keep your feet away from the rudder and your hands from the stick as I take off and land. Do you follow me?'

'Yes, sir.'

He summoned a mechanic who was standing by the tail. 'Did you start up this 'plane without chocks?'

'Yes, sir.'

'You've been here long enough to know about that. I don't want to crime you. See it doesn't happen again.'

'Very good, sir.'

He thought … *I shall think of this tomorrow, remember how I signed the test sheet, walked out, pulled on my parachute, saw my first pupil into his cockpit, reprimanded a mechanic. As I come out tomorrow, my mind busy with the details of my day's work, I shall remember this and another day will have passed.*

Aberdovey
November, 1935
February, 1936

Notes on the text

BY KATE MACDONALD AND DANIEL KILBURN

The First Chapter

beyond the bar: in deeper waters outside the lagoon that the sandbar protected.

Cader Idris: Cadair Idris is a mountain at the south of the Snowdonia National Park in Gwynedd, west Wales, looking down on the estuary with Barmouth at its mouth, and Arthog, where Rhys would be buried, on the southern bank of the estuary.

Service life: officers in the RAF during the interwar period only had a limited period of service, after which they were required to return to civilian life.

lifeboat slip: the slipway from which the lifeboat would be launched.

dead reckoning: navigating by planning the intended route by compass bearing, taking into account the airspeed, time and drift modified for wind speed and direction.

altimeter: an instrument for measuring height from the ground.

CFS: the Central Flying School of the Royal Air Force where Service instructors were trained.

get steam up: RAF slang for getting angry, analogous to a contemporary railway engine in that the Committee would turn red as if too hot and spout steam, ready to make a loud noise.

kites: planes, possibly after one of the first successful British biplanes from 1910, nicknamed the Boxkite. Early planes were made of canvas and wood, much like a child's kite.

flips: flights.

dual: lessons in a dual control training aircraft.

split-arse: analogous to 'the seat of one's pants', ie flying or behaving recklessly and probably dangerously.

shoot-up: literally, to fly in low with all guns blazing; figuratively, as here, to fly or otherwise behave in a way intended to impress anyone watching. Could also mean to get very drunk.

stalled: when an aeroplane wing is no longer able to generate enough lift for controlled flight (due to low speed or high angle-of-attack) and the plane subsequently drops towards the ground.

put on bank: tilt the aircraft by lowering one wing.

spinning: when the aeroplane descends by spinning (yawing) around its vertical axis because one wing has stalled more than the other, resulting in either decreasing, or complete loss of, control.

ailerons: hinged control surfaces in the wings that alter the angle or roll of the wing, allowing the aircraft to bank.

The Second Chapter

sidcot: a flying suit overall, worn over day clothes or uniform.

apron: the concreted area leading from runway to hangers.

doped: aircraft in this period had canvas wings that needed treatment with 'dope', a flammable nitrocelluloid paint that would tauten the material to reduce friction and drag. Too much would reduce aerodynamic efficiency.

GE: a licenced ground engineer. In this case it means Perkins specifically, as the only properly licenced engineer in the Club.

cheese-cutter: the elevator trim, controlling the compensating fore and aft movement of the aircraft against the horizontal of the ground.

Sutton harness: a safety harness with a quick release mechanism.

airscrew: the blades of the plane propellor.

Meyrowitz goggles: a high-quality brand of flying goggles to protect the eyes.

force land: a forced landing or an emergency landing under full control of whatever equipment is still working.

types: aircraft designers produced different types that were modifications of the same basic design.

take a woman there: a live-in landlady would object to overnight stays by women, as this could imply her premises were being used for prostitution.

Rabelaisian jokes: scatological, vulgar and/or sexual jokes.

initialled a bar chit: running a tab on drinks and meals that would be presented as a monthly bill.

RAF Reserve flying school: many British aircraft companies in the 1930s ran Reserve flying schools for the Air Ministry to give practice and more experience to 'weekend pilots' in the RAF Reserve.

prize raspberry: got told off thoroughly, in this case with good reason.

head-in-the-bag: slang for instrument flying instruction with a hood over the pupil's cockpit, to remove external observations as if flying in cloud, for example.

Sopwith, and Grahame-White and Hamel and Fleming: aviation pioneer and aircraft designer Sir Thomas Sopwith (1888–1989); Claude Grahame-White (1879–1959) made the first night flight and led the first night patrol in September 1914; Gustav Hamel (1889–1914) was a pioneering pilot in flight records and aerobatics. Fleming might be Clifford Fleming-Williams (1880–1940), a pioneer in hydro-aircraft and aircraft design before the First World War.

ack emmas: RAF slang for air mechanics.

Gosport tube: communications system between pilot and passenger or co-pilot, with rubber tubes running along the fuselage.

The Fourth Chapter

ab initio: Latin, 'from the beginning', in this case a beginner; still used to indicate the path or training required for a novice pilot to achieve a particular licence.

slots: slots, or slats, are devices fitted to some Tiger Moth wings to improve lift at low speed and during aerobatics.

The Fifth Chapter

RAFO: The Reserve of Air Force Officers, established by the Air Ministry as a way of building up a pool of pilots in case of the by now impending war.

RPM: engine revolutions per minute.

C G Grey: Charles Grey Grey, founder and editor of *The Aeroplane* magazine until 1939.

The Sixth Chapter

FTS: a flying training school.

ASI: air-speed indicator.

blood wagon: ambulance.

longeron: part of the inner fuselage structure or frame, bearing load along the length of the aircraft.

The Seventh Chapter

Oxford Group: a Christian organisation founded by Frank Buchman who believed, among other things, that the solution to overcoming fear was to submit one's life to God's plan.

The Ninth Chapter

PBI: Poor Bloody Infantry, the regular army.

The Tenth Chapter

miss so much: in the original Hawkings says an extra phrase, ', like Jews and niggers', which has been excised in this edition.

πάντα ῥεῖ: 'panta rhei' is a phrase from the Greek philosopher Heraclitus, meaning 'everything flows' or 'all things are in flux'. In this context it probably means something like 'everything changes'. (With thanks to Emer O'Hanlon.)

The Twelfth Chapter

Self: a melodramatic novel from 1922 about sex and betrayal. Nichols would move on from this style to far greater success as a writer of semi-autobiographical waspish comedies in horticultural settings.

The Thirteenth Chapter

BNC: Brasenose College, University of Oxford.

The Fourteenth Chapter

Blake: the quotation is from the last chapter of *Jerusalem. The Emanation of the Giant Albion*, one of William Blake's